An Insubstantial Pageant

By the same author

The Golden Songbird
Madalena
The Sergeant Major's Daughter
A Fine Silk Purse
The Incomparable Miss Brady
The Rose Domino
A Highly Respectable Marriage
The Runaway Bride

An Insubstantial Pageant

Sheila Walsh

Century Publishing
London

First published in Great Britain in 1986 by
Century Hutchinson Ltd,
Brookmount House, 62–65 Chandos Place,
Covent Garden, London WC2N 4NW

ISBN 0 7126 9420 X

Typeset by Inforum Ltd, Portsmouth
Printed in Great Britain by
Anchor Brendon Ltd, Tiptree, Essex

For my lovely, long-suffering husband

Our revels now are ended. These our actors,
As I foretold you, were all spirits and
Are melted into air, into thin air:
And, like the baseless fabric of this vision,
The cloud-capp'd towers, the gorgeous palaces,
The solemn temples, the great globe itself,
Yea, all which it inherit, shall dissolve
And, like this insubstantial pageant faded,
Leave not a rack behind. We are such stuff
As dreams are made on, and our little life
Is rounded with a sleep.

The Tempest Act IV, sc. i

Prologue

The Schloss Bayersdorf stood on a rock at the head of a steep wooded gorge with its curious assortment of turrets bathed in sunshine and the formidable mountain ranges of Bohemia marching in serried ranks at its back. It looked for all the world like something out of a mythical romance. Which in a sense it was, for the tiny principality of Gellenstadt, ruled by the house of Bayersdorf from medieval times and in size no bigger than many an English country estate, was by its very situation cut off from the world. So much so that, although technically annexed by Bonaparte, it had escaped the fate of its more prestigious neighbours, being deemed of little use to anyone – its only claim to singularity being the exquisite silverware for which it was famed.

It was hot that afternoon and the long windows of the throne room were flung open in an effort to trap whatever fresh air might be found. But the fine muslin curtains scarcely moved, and for Grand Prince Adolphus each breath was a small agony . . .

He stood with his back to the room, the set of his shoulders proclaiming a man of stern disciplines – an impression confirmed by the rigid conformity of his dress which allowed of no concession to the heat. It was therefore some considerable measure of his discomfort that one hand occasionally moved unobstrusively to tug at the high tight collar of his coat as though in a vain attempt to ease his breathing.

The furtive movement did not escape the notice of the young lady occupying the ornamental sofa nearby. Baroness Lottie Raimund contemplated that tortured yet still handsome profile with veiled concern, noting how cruelly the light slanting across it emphasized the mask of hauteur which so effectively kept people at a distance (though it had never done so with her); it emphasized too the Prince's growing frailty, the ravages wrought by pain, which a trim, greying beard imperfectly concealed.

But she permitted no hint of her disquiet to cloud the smiling eyes lifted to him in candid speculation as he turned at last to speak.

The Grand Prince allowed himself the luxury of dwelling for a brief moment on their warmth.

They were lovely eyes, he mused, irresistibly moved as always by the perpetual evocation of spring in their purple-blue depths – a kind of rich velvety texture which mirrored almost exactly the vivid gentians that carpeted the slopes above the Schloss each year in early March, and which he doubted he would live to see again. The realization, catching him for once off-guard, threatened his hard-won acceptance. Ah, why was it always the small things that got beneath one's skin? He almost groaned the words aloud.

But the moment of weakness was ruthlessly quashed, the only evidence of its passing an involuntary tightening of the mouth which might as easily be attributed to a spasm of physical pain.

'Forgive me, Charlotte,' he began with the old-fashioned formality of address that had always made it difficult for him to accept the more familiar diminutive of her name. 'You must be wondering why I have sent for you?'

Lottie knew perfectly well what, or more accurately who, had prompted the interview, but she had wisdom enough not to say so, preferring rather to try if she could to tease him out of his obvious preoccupation with pain.

'Indeed, sire. I have spent the whole of my journey here in a quake, racking my brains for evidence of recent misdemeanours!'

She was granted the satisfaction of drawing from him a faint abstracted smile as he continued: 'This Peace Congress they are to hold in Vienna shortly – my mother tells me you have a mind to attend it?'

Lottie swallowed the retort which sprang impetuously to her lips, choosing her words with care, speaking lightly.

'I fear that Her Serene Highness does not approve my decision. She feels that young ladies, even widows of unimpeachable virtue –' she almost added the damning 'English-born', but thought better of it ' – should not, in Her Serene Highness' judgement, go unprotected into such fast company as will most certainly be gathered there.' Her expressive eyes invited him to enjoy with her the comic absurdity of such a view, and when he did not immediately do so, she said with determined good humour, 'Do you mean to censure me also?'

'My dear Charlotte,' he said with considerably less constraint, 'it is not for me to approve or disapprove. You must know that you are at perfect liberty to go wherever you please without applying to me for permission.'

'Why, so I had supposed.' She hesitated, aware that he had stopped short of saying more. 'Yet you do not quite like the idea of my going, I think?'

'Would you heed me if I said that I did not?' he asked dryly.

A rueful smile curved Lottie's mouth. 'I would not care to incur your displeasure.'

'An equivocal reply, my dear . . . eminently worthy of a diplomat's daughter.' But an answering smile softened the severity of his features, robbing the words of much of their irony. 'However, I repeat it is not for me to presume to censure you. I haven't the right, and in any case there will be many people coming out from England to attend the Congress and it would be quite wrong in me to deny you the opportunity of meeting them and perhaps renewing old acquaintances.' His shoulders lifted in a gesture of resignation. 'It is more than two years since your husband died. I am only too aware that there is little to hold you here now.'

'But I love Gellenstadt! It has been my home for the last eight years . . . the only settled home I can remember!' Lottie rose, the soft peach-bloom silk of her skirts billowing as she moved swiftly across the room, her hands extended in a gesture of supplication. 'It *is* only a visit I intend, truly.'

'Yes, of course.' The Prince took the hands she held out to him, feeling as always the curious sensation of strength that seemed to flow into him from her warm yielding clasp. He tried not to think how he would continue to exist while she was away, without the constant encouragement her presence gave to him.

'Eight years is a long time,' he said slowly.

'A lifetime,' she agreed. 'I frequently ponder upon how different my life might have been if poor dear Otto had not so gallantly offered me the protection of his name when Papa died in that tragic accident. I can still remember quite vividly how I felt – trying so hard to be sensible – willing myself not to give way to that terrible feeling of panic as I faced the prospect of being entirely alone in the world, for we had nothing in the way of close family, you know.'

A convulsive tightening of his fingers caused her to look him straight in the eyes. What she saw there would have daunted anyone else, but she continued doggedly. 'But you *did* know, didn't you? Somehow you guessed exactly how I felt. I have never voiced the thought until now, but whenever I do dwell upon my good fortune it becomes more and more obvious that Otto, good sweet man though he was, would never have dreamed of offering for me, had he not been prompted to do so . . . from a higher authority, perhaps?'

The Prince pursed his lips, his hauteur now very evident. 'You have a fertile imagination, my dear. Otto was devoted to you.'

Lottie chuckled. 'Ah, now it is you who are being equivocal, sire. But I won't press the matter. In truth, I have been more than contented with my lot.'

He released her hands, relieved that he was not obliged to dissemble further. He might, under pressure, have found it exceedingly difficult to convince her that his then Secretary of State, though the most amiable of men, had not taken a certain amount of persuading before he could be brought to relinquish his comfortable bachelor existence at a relatively advanced age in order to secure Charlotte's future.

He had convinced himself at the time that he must accept responsibility for Sir Charles Weston's untimely death, which had happened on a hunting trip arranged for his pleasure while he was engaged in a diplomatic visit to Gellenstadt in that winter of 1805 . . . and, likewise, for the seventeen year old Charlotte who had been so sadly orphaned. But if he was honest he had been captivated by Charlotte from the start, and could not bear the thought of her returning to England, perhaps for good.

How different his own life might have been had he then found the courage to defy the outraged sensibilities of his mother and the disapproval of those closest to him in order to marry Charlotte himself. But the reserve in his own nature – a curse from childhood – and his strong sense of what he owed to his position had held him silent. And Charlotte had married Otto Raimund.

'I can still remember the first time I saw you,' he said involuntarily. '*Jungfer Husch*, I called you – our "miss in a hurry"!'

'Oh, yes!' This time her laugh spilled out, echoing round the throne room with a flagrant disregard for its vaulted splendour, flirting among the ancient tapestries like a much-needed breath of fresh air. 'Such a great lump of a girl I was then – all arms and legs and awkwardness – always wanting to ride everywhere *ventre-à-terre!* Papa must have despaired of me many a time!'

'On the contrary, Sir Charles was quite inordinately proud of you. It was evident whenever he spoke of you. He told me once that you warmed his spirit . . .'

'Papa said that?' she asked softly.

Prince Adolphus inclined his head. 'And I know exactly what he meant, for I too was aware of that quality in you from the very first. You are the only person I think, who never once stood in awe of me.' His mouth quirked in a self-deprecating way. 'That may not seem of importance to you, but for me in those early days it was a revelation. There was then – and still is in you a great openness of character – a capacity to interest yourself quite genuinely in other people to a degree that transcends mere curiosity –'

'Please!' she begged in blushing confusion. But it was a long speech for so shy a man, and she would not offend him for the world. 'Indeed, it is more than kind of you to account as a virtue what most people might regard as interference . . . and to not so much as hint at my unbiddable temper which still occasionally leads me to say more than I ought!'

'Oh, that!' He dismissed it. 'A show of spirit is no bad thing once in a while –' he smiled faintly '– and you are always full of remorse afterwards.'

As she stood quiescent, with the laughter still lingering in her eyes, it was difficult for him to equate the slender elegant creature in her stylish high-waisted dress with that merry madcap of old. She was a little on the tall side for a woman, confident and graceful in her movements, the girlish plumpness long gone. Marriage to Otto, himself a man of great style, had done much for her. But there were still glimpses of that other Charlotte in the vivid mobile features – in her generous mouth with its full, deliciously curvaceous lower lip. And in her rich red hair, the luxuriant tumble of curls having long since given place to a fashionable fringe, and in her eyes – something she was probably quite unaware of – a curious innocence that belied all the rest.

The Prince sighed. 'I could wish that my Sophia had a little of your strength of character.'

Lottie felt a spurt of indignation as she thought of the grave young girl, on the brink of beauty, but shy like her father, with any tendencies to forwardness swiftly repressed by a too-strict governess, at the instigation no doubt of her grandmother.

'Oh, how unjust!' she exclaimed. 'Your daughter doesn't want for character. I admit that she is something of an air-dreamer at present, but I daresay that comes of being rather too sheltered from life.' She longed to say more, but now was not the time. She contented herself with saying warmly, 'Sophia is in many ways a very young seventeen, but she has a lot of good qualities.'

'She also has a stalwart champion in you, my dear,' he said dryly. He smiled briefly and turned back to the window once more. 'In point of fact, it is of Sophia that I really wished to speak. I'm sure that you are right when you say that she has been overprotected – losing her mother so early in her life – my own mother's influence . . .'

His shoulders stiffened perceptibly, though whether from pain or merely painful memory Lottie couldn't be sure. When he presently continued his voice was firm.

'But all that must now change. A husband will have to be found for her.'

Lottie stared. 'My dear sir, you cannot mean to catapult the child straight from the schoolroom into marriage. It would be too cruel.'

'She is the same age as you were when –'

'My case was different! Oh, surely there is plenty of time for Sophia?'

There was a small silence. Then: 'For Sophia, perhaps,' he said quietly.

Fear jolted her, tightening its grip on her stomach. She moved forward to lay an urgent hand on his arm.

'Your health is not worse?'

'No worse than usual.'

'Then how dare you frighten me so?' she cried.

He turned his head. His eyes sought hers and found them bright, with chips of anger masking a greater fear.

'It would be absurd, however, to assume that time is on my side,' he said steadily. 'There are, besides, so many uncertainties here . . .' He stopped abruptly and covered her hand with his. 'Come, I am only seeking to ensure that my daughter will be safe, should anything happen to me. That is surely the very least that a father can do?'

'And happy, too. Sophia must be happy as well as safe!'

'Yes, of course.' His voice betrayed a hint of irritability, as though he were tiring fast. 'I am not insensitive, I hope. The matter I wished to broach – and it seems to be taking an unconscionable time to come to the purpose of our talk – is, whether you think the Congress would make a suitable venue for Sophia to make her curtsy to the world?'

He had succeeded in surprising her. 'It would be ideal,' she said. 'After all, where else could one hope to find so many of Europe's finest families gathered together?'

'That is what I thought,' he mused.

'So you have decided to come to Vienna, too, sire. I couldn't be more pleased!'

The Prince held up a hand. 'No, I had hoped, but it will not now be possible.'

He made no attempt to enlarge upon his reasons, but it would not be difficult to hazard a guess, Lottie felt. Quite apart from his precarious state of health, there had been one or two instances of unrest in Gellenstadt recently which, though not serious of themselves, might well make him reluctant to be away. But if the Prince did not wish to undertake his daughter's coming out in person . . . Something in the way he was looking at her caused Lottie's eyes to widen in sudden realization.

'You would entrust Sophia to my charge?'

'I can think of no one better suited, though I am aware that it is asking a great deal of you.' He silenced the denial that rose spontaneously to her lips, unable quite to hide the bleakness in his voice. 'It is a sobering reflection that you probably understand my daughter better than I do – better than any of us do, in fact. However, I appreciate that such an arrangement might place unacceptable restrictions upon your freedom. You will need time to consider . . .'

'Oh no! It would give me the greatest pleasure to have Sophia with me, but –' Lottie's mind was racing, still adjusting to the idea. 'Have you fully considered . . . Her Serene Highness won't like it. She will think me too young . . . not sufficiently high-born . . .'

'I will deal with my mother,' he said with clipped formality, though a curious light blazed in his eyes. 'So? You will do this for me, Charlotte?'

Her answering smile was a little bemused. 'Yes, of course, sire. I am honoured that you should ask me.'

'Good.' The word seemed like a sigh. He was about to leave his place at the window when a movement below caught his eye, in the angle of the building where the walls of the east wing cast their heavy shadow. A moment later his brother Paul emerged into the light, moving with cat-like grace across the sun-drenched courtyard. The assurance, the contained power of Paul's lithe figure seemed to the prince to underline not only his own growing physical inadequacy, but also the urgent necessity to resolve those issues which lay so oppressively on his mind. So much to be done, and so little time . . . The dry cough that was seldom absent these days shook his neat elegant frame and was only partially stifled by the handkerchief he pressed quickly to his mouth.

Lottie was at his side in an instant, scolding him for standing so long when he ought to be resting as she led him, unresisting, to a high-backed wing chair. Once settled, he leaned his head against the cushion she placed for him and closed his eyes against the bitter frustration of finding himself trapped more and more in too feeble a body. Unaware in his misery of how much his face revealed, he listened vaguely to the faint rustle of Lottie's skirts, and the chink of glass on glass as she poured some of his cordial.

When she returned to his side, he said, without opening his eyes, and without any longer troubling to hide his weariness, 'There is one other favour I would ask of you – before we are interrupted . . .'

Nothing of Lottie's panic showed in her voice. 'You know that I will do anything you ask, but please to drink this first.'

He opened his eyes and took the glass she held out to him. 'About Vienna . . .' he began.

'Drink,' she said firmly.

A faint smile lit his eyes as he complied, though it faded almost immediately.

'The matter does concern Sophia insofar as she is my heir. As you know, the house of Bayersdorf has always descended through the female line where necessary – and it is my overriding concern that Gellenstadt should still be here for her to inherit.'

'Oh, but surely . . .' she protested.

'It is by no means inevitable, my dear Charlotte. You, of all people, must know that . . . know, too, that my present Secretary of State is not half the man your late husband was . . .'

Lottie remained silent, for she could not but share his misgivings about the swaggering Count von Deiter.

'Also,' the tired voice continued, 'he is too much under my brother's influence. Paul, I need hardly tell you, cherishes ambitions for Gellenstadt's future which do not accord with my own. And I feel sure that Paul means to go to Vienna.' He drew a painful breath, but brushed aside her protestations that all this would keep for another day. 'No, let me finish. Bonaparte's entire empire will be in the melting pot at the Congress, and like it or not, we are a part of it. Political chicanery and double dealing will be rife, and small states like Gellenstadt will be mere pawns in the game.'

Lottie watched the Prince anxiously, but he seemed to be breathing more easily now, sipping his cordial reflectively, as though searching for the right words. 'What I really need, of course,' he mused, 'is someone – a kind of ally at court, if you like – to keep a discreet eye on my brother's doings at Vienna, someone who can move freely in the same circles and has some knowledge of the diplomatic world.'

He watched enlightenment struggle with disbelief in her lovely eyes. Then a splutter of amused outrage escaped her.

'If you mean what I think you mean, sire, it is the most impossible, the most nonsensical suggestion I ever heard!'

'I can't agree. It is the world you know best, the world you grew up in, and as Sophia's chaperone you would be ideally placed to observe both Paul and von Deiter . . .'

Lottie was walking about the room in an agitated manner. 'Your brother would be furious if he found out . . .'

'Found out what? My dear Charlotte, you are to have the care of my daughter. What could be more natural, since I cannot be there myself, than that you should write to me from time to time with news, both general and particular, pertaining to Gellenstadt? You might even, should the occasion arise, see your way to dropping a word in the right ear, while you are there – to further the cause of independence for Gellenstadt.'

She came to a halt at last, standing over him. 'Prince Adolphus Ludovic Wilhelm, you are a devious man. Don't pretend to me that this is a spur of the moment idea. Bring Sophia out, indeed!' She tried to look severe, but her eyes were already sparkling. 'You would be well served if I refused to play your little game.'

'But you won't,' he said calmly, observing her reactions over the rim of his glass and already looking less grey. 'I am concerned for Sophia – yes, but I am concerned for you, also. Do you suppose I have not been acutely aware of your growing ennui these past months? Idleness is not conducive to a nature such as yours, yet you have been obliged to kick your heels here ever since Otto's death, watching his successor make a botch of much that you achieved together. It is high time you put your talents to some use again.'

'So I am to turn spy for you . . . is that it?'

The Prince looked prim. 'My dear Charlotte, how melodramatic you make it sound. You were going to Vienna, whether or no. I merely ask you to employ your not inconsiderable capacity for observation to good account while you are there. What, pray, is there to quarrel with in that?'

'What indeed?' Lottie flung back her head with a laugh of pure merriment.

It was this joyously infectious sound that greeted Her Serene

Highness, the Dowager Grand Princess Wilhelmina Louise, as a lackey threw open the doors of the throne room to admit her. But the sound evoked little response in the stiffly regal breast as the old lady stomped down the room towards them, leaning heavily on a stout gold-topped stick. Pride blazed from the pale eyes set in a craze of sallow wrinkles that clung tenaciously to her strong high cheekbones – the only enduring evidence of a once-handsome face.

Her Serene Highness' own rigid adherence to protocol was unyielding. She was therefore outraged by the discovery of this young woman, whom she had always disliked, thus familiarly closeted with her son and exhibiting the free and easy manners which clearly marked her down as a person of little consequence. She came to a halt, fixing Lottie with her cold basilisk stare.

'Baroness. I was not informed that you were here.' Her words, rapier-tipped, jabbed the air. 'I came to speak with my son.'

Lottie threw a quick rueful glance at Prince Adolphus, who had sworn softly at his mother's untimely entrance. He now stood, looking equally cold and withdrawn. It was at moments like this that the likeness between them was most marked. Lottie made a conscious effort to subdue the almost childish fury that the Dowager Princess so often managed to arouse in her.

'Then I will not inconvenience your Serene Highness by remaining,' she said as pleasantly as she could manage. 'I was on the point of leaving anyway.' Aware that it would be commented upon if she did not, she dipped a brief curtsy to the Prince, saying quietly as she did so: 'I assume that Sophia is as yet unaware of your intentions? I will say nothing until you have spoken to her.'

She curtsied with exquisite correctness to the old lady and was about to depart when the sharp voice halted her.

'One moment, Baroness.' She had held stubbornly to this formal mode of address from the day of Lottie's marriage to Baron Raimund, prior to which she had not deigned to notice her at all. 'I would know exactly what it is that my son intends for Sophia, and how it comes to pass that you are privy to it before her own grandmother?'

'Later, Mother,' said the Prince repressively. 'Go along now, Charlotte. And thank you.'

The royal cane rapped the floor imperatively. 'Not later, Adolphus. Now. And I prefer that the Baroness remain, since she is apparently closely concerned in the matter.'

Already, in a matter of moments, the Dowager Princess had reduced her son to a renewed bout of coughing which she suffered with a kind of contained impatience, making no effort to go to his aid. Lottie swallowed on the hot words that rose to her lips and moved swiftly but without fuss to pick up the glass of cordial which he had laid aside. She put it into his hand.

'My thanks,' he gasped. 'But . . . go now. I shall do well enough.' Perspiration beaded his brow and he dabbed at it with his handkerchief.

'Will you let me send for your man?' she begged him, half scolding. 'This heat is not good for you. You should be resting properly in your room.'

'No, no. See – I am better already.' His smile was meant to reassure her, but the effort it cost him only made her more angry.

'Well, at least sit down – and try not to talk.' Lottie watched him hesitate, glance in his mother's direction. She swung round, exasperation making her incautious. 'Please – if your Serene Highness would sit?' And when the old lady declined to heed her, she lowered her voice. 'Ma'am, I beg of you! You must know that he will not sit while you remain standing!'

Hatred flared momentarily in the Princess' eyes, but was quickly brought under control.

'Thank you, Baroness. I hope I know what is best for my son.' Her cold glance flicked across to the distressed Prince. 'Oh, for pity's sake, Adolphus, sit down. If there is one thing I cannot abide, it is self-imposed martyrdom!'

Lottie was so incensed that she could hardly bear to look as he stiffened, then shrugged and resumed his seat, propping his head on one slim hand. The Princess, however, had already transferred her attention back to Lottie.

'I have changed my mind, Baroness. I will accept your apology, and then you may leave us.'

Uncomfortably aware that she had gone beyond the bounds of what was acceptable, Lottie was by now too angry to heed the inner voice that preached caution. 'Surely what you have to say could wait?' she exclaimed. 'Cannot you see, ma'am, that Prince Adolphus is in no condition to withstand one of your inquisitions?'

There was a sharp hiss of indrawn breath, an unnerving silence. Then, in a voice quite awesome in its frigidity, 'I have said – *you may leave us.*'

She had gone much too far. She knew it. Yet even now Lottie was tempted to defy the Princess and remain. It would be courting folly with a vengeance, she knew, but in her present mood she cared little for that. In the end it was the Prince himself who decided the matter. He had straightened up and was regarding them both with a weary exasperation.

'No more, I beg you,' he sighed.

'Oh, very well – I *will* go!' Lottie cried, sketched a hasty curtsy, snatched up her discarded hat and reticule, and quit the room with inelegant haste. Her fingers clenched convulsively round the hat's stylish brim as the force of her emotions carried her on rushing feet along lofty corridors where satyrs leered and laughing cherubs leaned perilously down from the wide rococo frieze to watch her passing.

That old woman was a monster, she raged inwardly, an unfeeling, uncaring monster in whom pride was everything, duty was everything, discipline was everything! Small wonder that Prince Adolphus had grown such an impenetrable shell of reserve – any craving for affection must have been crushed out of him very early in his life. As for Prince Paul . . .

'Whither goest thou, O lady in a hurry?'

With uncanny timing the mocking voice cut across her teeming thoughts, breaking their thread. Her step faltered – and stopped. Prince Paul lounged in an open doorway watching her, his slim form outlined against the sunlight which streamed from the room behind him, creating a shimmering aura about his sun-bleached hair.

Lottie blinked and the handsome features swam into focus, their aristocratic symmetry marred by a proudly worn duelling scar that ran from his left temple to just below the cheekbone.

'I saw the patient Humbert walking your carriage in the courtyard as I came in.' He straightened up with graceful ease and stepped towards her. 'But what is this? Tears, lovely

Lottie? Now there's a thing! Who has been ruffling your feathers, I wonder? Not my big brother, I'll warrant.'

She had no doubt that he was trying to provoke her, but his lazy sarcasm acted as a brake rather than a spur. She drew a steadying breath and even managed a brittle laugh.

'With respect, Highness, it is none of your business.'

'True.' He grinned without malice. 'But you cannot deny me my curiosity. If I had to hazard a bet, my money would be on dear Mama – but clearly you don't mean to gratify me.' When she did not reply, he shrugged philosophically. 'Ah well, at least you will permit me to walk you to your carriage?' His fingers closed lightly on her arm.

'No, really, there isn't the least need,' she said quickly.

The pressure of his fingers increased fractionally. 'True again. But how dull life would be if we were governed solely by necessity.'

Lottie was not fooled by his air of sweet reason. She knew that further protest would serve only to make her appear churlish, and provide him with an excellent excuse for retaliation. So she acquiesced with what grace she could muster and fell into step beside him. It sometimes irked her that in the nine years she had known him, she had never quite learned how to cope with Prince Paul. At five and thirty, he was a good ten years younger than Adolphus, and so different from his brother in temperament that, had his mother been less of a high stickler, one might have been tempted to wonder. But the mere suspicion of any lapse from grace on the part of Her Serene Highness was enough to send one off into whoops! Lottie's mouth curved quite unconsciously just thinking about it. Paul's volatile temperament must, she concluded, stem from his father who had, if rumour were to be believed, been something of a rakehell.

Her smile had not gone unnoticed. Paul said casually, 'That's more the Lottie I expected to see, filled with happy anticipation. There is a strong rumour abroad that you are to go to Vienna this autumn?'

There seemed little point in denying it. 'I thought it might be amusing,' she said lightly.

Paul looked aslant at her with that lazy watchful smile. 'Are you then so sorely in need of amusement?'

She chose her words with care. 'Not particularly. But everyone is the better for a change occasionally.'

'Perhaps you should tell that to my esteemed brother,' he drawled. 'He grows devilish ill-tempered of late.'

'And so would you be if you were forced to endure such crippling ill health!' The retort was out before Lottie could prevent it, and it earned her a small cynical smile.

'My pardon. I tend to forget what a staunch champion Adolphus has in you, my dear.'

He hadn't forgotten, of course. His baiting had been quite deliberate and she had gratified him by rising to it. Lottie didn't know whether she was more angry with him or with herself, as she sought to regain some measure of composure. 'He gets little enough sympathy from his family,' she said quietly. And then, reverting pointedly to their earlier conversation, 'The fact is, I haven't been anywhere since Otto died, and am beginning to feel quite dull. So, where better than Vienna to give my thoughts a new direction? With so many people gathered there, lots of whom I shall know, I can hardly fail to find a little light diversion.'

'My dear Baroness, you make it sound positively irresistible!' he drawled. 'Who knows but that I may decide to join you there.'

It was on the tip of her tongue to blurt out that she had thought his mind already made up, but this time discretion won. They had reached the head of the main staircase, and here Prince Paul stopped, his glance shifting casually towards the upper floor where the schoolroom lay.

'You don't wish to see Sophia?'

His voice was smooth, his expression bland as his eyes met hers, slate grey and guileless, yet Lottie once again had the curious impression that he knew more than he ought, though she was at a loss to know how.

'I think not,' she said lightly. 'The Princess will be at her lessons, and Fräulein Lanner frowns upon interruptions.'

'Of course.'

Paul inclined his head with faint mockery and they proceeded in a silence that was something less than comfortable. In the courtyard Lottie's groom Humbert was quietly walking the horses up and down, a pale silky shadow at his side. The little spaniel moved forward and then stopped uncertainly upon seeing that her mistress was not alone.

'Come, Tasha,' she said quietly as Humbert approached the door of the open barouche and let down the steps. But the dog continued to hover nervously watching until Lottie was settled in her place before leaping up under the amused gaze of Prince Paul to nestle close into her skirts.

'I trust the bitch does not reflect the sentiments of her mistress,' he mused with an ironical smile, and then as she blushed his smile widened into something altogether different, and he raised her hand to his lips. 'Until Vienna.'

Lottie contained her feelings until the carriage had negotiated the steeply winding road that traversed the ancient bridge with the river rushing past below, and had turned down past the unprepossessing cluster of buildings where the famous Gellenstadt silver had been fashioned for generations, the skill passed on from father to son.

When the road reached a fork, she leaned forward and asked Humbert to stop. She stepped down, snapping her fingers for Tasha to do likewise.

'Take the carriage home,' she told Humbert. 'I need some fresh air and exercise.'

The coachman received this uncalled-for explanation with a stolid 'Ja, Baroness,' which managed to incorporate within its brevity that he was well-used to her odd ways, and that it was no business of his if she wished to expose herself to the gruelling heat of the afternoon. He contented himself with a final gruff 'You should wear your hat,' before, with a click of tongue and teeth, he gathered the reins and set his horses in motion again.

The implied reproof dispelled much of Lottie's irritation and brought a faint smile. Otto's servants were devoted to her to a man, she knew, but they were not above treating her occasionally as though she were still that rather harum-scarum girl who had come years ago to shatter their ordered existence.

It was very quiet when the rumble of the carriage wheels had died away. Not a soul to be seen – and small wonder for the deep valley, which could act as a funnel when the wind blew, soon became a cauldron in the summer's heat, in spite of the water that rushed unceasingly past in the ravine below. The sun's relentless rays beat back at her from the road and as her neck felt the instant impact, she hastily donned the chip straw hat whose brim she had so impetuously ruined. Tying the jonquil ribbons absent-mindedly under her chin, she sought the shade of the gigantic beech trees which seemed to grow straight out of the rocks. Across the river, black pines marched along the ridge and as she looked back the palace turrets shimmered in the heat haze with here and there on the distant mountain peaks the glitter of perpetual snow.

A faint rumble reminded her that somewhere beneath her, men were busy mining the silver that was so necessary to the continuity of Gellenstadt's fine traditions.

But how long could it last, she wondered, this preservation of exclusivity to which Prince Adolphus was so dedicated? If anything were to happen to him (and please God it would not!), for how long could the valley escape the threat of exploitation by stronger, more ambitious neighbours like Bavaria?

Prince Paul had never made any secret of the fact that he would like to see Gellenstadt as part of a much wider alliance, with more say in European affairs, and there were now many younger men in the valley, men who had formed a small company raised by Paul to fight with the Allied Armies against Napoleon, who echoed his ambitions. They had seen a world beyond their tiny homeland, and were no longer content to resume their former narrow existence.

For her own part Lottie was torn. Her heart was with Adolphus. She loved Gellenstadt the way it was and all her emotional instincts favoured keeping the *status quo*, but the practical side of her nature reluctantly acknowledged that some measure of participation in a wider spectrum of affairs could only benefit the lives of families in the valley. Even Otto, who was very much Adolphus' man and whose opinions she had so valued, had doubted the wisdom of holding aloof from the world and not long before his death had voiced hopes of persuading his Prince to look outward once the conflict was ended.

Lottie's smile was rueful as she turned at last to retrace her steps. The more she thought about it, the clearer it became that her visit to Vienna, so innocently conceived, was destined to be quite different from the uncomplicated holiday she had planned.

1

'Dear Baroness Lottie – do come and see! The Czar has left the Hofburg and will be passing beneath our window at any moment with all his retinue!'

The tremulous young voice wafting back through the open window from the balcony beyond was tinged with a kind of awe that made Lottie smile. Could this really be the subdued girl who had left Gellenstadt less than a week ago weighed down with exhortations from all sides as to what was expected of the heir to the principality? Fortunately the royal reserve had not been proof against the magic of Vienna, for the Princess had instantly succumbed like any country girl on her first visit to a glittering city – which in fact was exactly what she was.

'Not another procession,' said Lottie, with a sigh of mock resignation. 'I vow they do little else!'

This brought a little skirl of excited protestation, as Princess Sophia urged: 'Oh, do hurry or you will miss the best of it!'

With an amused shrug Lottie laid aside her embroidery and rose to weave her way among the grand and glorious superabundance of gilded furniture scattered indiscriminately about the spacious salon. To be sure, it was no hardship to do the Princess' bidding, for like Sophia she was already finding the preliminary social skirmishing of this Congress highly enjoyable. Tasha, basking in a pool of sunlight, lifted her head, opening one eye to watch her pass, then having satisfied herself that her mistress was not about to leave the room, allowed her silky ears to sink once more into the luxurious warmth of the Aubusson carpet.

Lottie chuckled to herself remembering Prince Adolphus' displeasure upon learning that an apartment was the best accommodation that his agent had been able to secure for them. Only the assurance that its appointments were more than adequate and that it occupied a prime position almost within sight of the Hofburg, where Emperor Francis was designated to play host to no less than an emperor and his empress, four kings, one queen, two hereditary princes, three grand duchesses and three princes of the blood, had persuaded him to acquiesce.

The agent had not exaggerated. In size and grandeur it might almost rival the Schloss Bayersdorf, comprising as it did a considerable portion of a huge sprawling mansion whose imposing facade would not have disgraced a full-scale palace, complete with many tall windows which allowed the light to flood in upon a cornucopia of lavishly decorated rooms where laughing rococo cherubs scattered plaster roses with indiscriminate generosity across compartmented ceilings, and friezes were a riot of swags and acanthus leaves!

What the agent had omitted to tell the Prince was that a shabby central stairway of noble proportions linked them quite publicly not only with a similar apartment, as yet vacant, which took up the other half of the first and second floors of the building, but also with less imposing accommodation on the floor above, to say nothing of a fraternity of musicians who inhabited the many minute attics set high up in the steep gables, or the even odder community of cheerful Viennese to be found in the labyrinth of basements.

Fräulein Lanner, already jealous of Lottie's authority, had been quick to express her outrage at the prospect of the Princess being exposed to all the *Hausparteien* in this odious way; there were even mutterings of murder and abductions.

'Nonsense!' Lottie had retorted, not troubling to hide her amusement. 'It can do Her Royal Highness nothing but good to see how others go on. For far too long she has been over-protected!'

Sophia was indeed entranced by all she saw, but Lottie did occasionally wonder if it had been quite wise further to alienate the governess. Her – 'As you will, Baroness – the decision is not for me to make,' had been subdued enough at the time, but there had been a barely detectable undertone of vehemence in the bitten-off words that seemed to have been reflected in the woman's subsequent behaviour.

Still, thought Lottie, no good ever came of worrying.

The sound of clattering hooves greeted her as she stepped out onto the balcony, to be immediately dazzled by the sight of

Alexander, Czar of Russia, with a smile on his little curving mouth, exuding an air of magnanimous nobility as he rode at the head of the jingling cavalcade which trotted past in a vivid kaleidoscope of colour. The mellow autumn sun glanced with blinding brilliance off polished cuirasses, and feathered plumes nodded in strict time to the hoofbeats. But Alexander outshone them all. His tall figure was encased in a dark green uniform whose short-skirted tunic with its high gold collar was so padded and heavily laced that his arms appeared to hang stiffly like a doll's beneath the gilded epaulets.

'He looks like a big, benign angel!' she murmured irreverently, but the words evoked no response. Sophia was in another world, and who could blame her? There was a total absence of reality about these increasing attempts by important personages to outdo one another in magnificence which should render them absurd, but as yet they merely constituted an irresistible attraction so that it came as no surprise to Lottie to find the blood beginning to tingle in her own veins in a way she hadn't experienced in years, filling her with the kind of giddy emotions that ought more properly to belong to a girl of Sophia's age!

'Oh, see!' Sophia's fingers closed impetuously on her arm. 'Is that not Prince Metlin in the place of honour beside the Czar? Yes, I am sure it is – one would know those splendid red-gold whiskers anywhere!' Her sigh held a wealth of meaning. 'How handsome he is!'

Heavens! thought Lottie. And this after only one meeting!

'Who . . . the Czar or Prince Metlin?' she quizzed her eager young companion, knowing the answer full well. Sophia's trill of laughter merely confirmed it.

Lottie was unsure whether to laugh with her, or scold. Sophia had been repressed for so long that a part of her rejoiced to witness such joyous spontaneity. In her opinion a girl of seventeen, even a princess, should have all the world before her, a myriad experiences to introduce her to life and love, even a little – just a very little – heartbreak, and how was that possible with Fräulein Lanner constantly preaching propriety and fostering the child's natural reserve, deeming it a mark of her true station in life?

It was at this point in her reflections that Lottie intercepted an impudent grin directed upwards with practised precision by the Colonel Prince in acknowledgement of the petite royal personage leaning with such perilous enthusiasm from the balcony above, and in turning to observe its effect on Sophia, she experienced her first twinge of misgiving. For there was a stillness, a kind of absorbed dreaminess in the profile thus presented to her, one glossy brown curl lying carelessly across a flawless cheek – a profile whose sketchy delicacy already showed promise of great beauty. As the Czar's retinue disappeared from view, Sophia flung a brief shining glance that made Lottie's heart turn over, bringing home to her with disturbing clarity the true enormity of the task she had so lightly undertaken.

Sophia was such an innocent. Please God she did not mean to lose her heart to the first amiable rogue who showed a disposition to flirt with her.

They had met Prince Metlin for the first time on the previous evening at one of the many glittering informal assemblies already proliferating throughout Vienna although the Congress was not yet officially under way. The young man's charm was undeniable, the frankness of his admiration engaging, yet Lottie knew that neither his nobility of rank nor his exceeding amiability was likely to make him one whit more acceptable to Prince Adolphus as a serious suitor for his daughter's hand. Nor for one moment did she suppose that his ambitions lay in that direction, since for all his gallantry towards Sophia, he had quite blatantly indicated his willingness to extend the same favour to her.

She put the thought from her and addressed herself to the dreaming girl.

'Sophia, I really do think we should go in now.' She tried to sound severe. 'Ladies do not under any circumstances disport themselves on balconies for all the world to see.'

'I know, but I am discovering that it is fun to occasionally do what one should not!' There was a delightful hint of mischief in the way Sophia's straight, artistocratic nose wrinkled up though she turned obediently enough to leave. On the point of so doing, however, her attention was drawn to a sudden stir created by a pair of carriages drawing up below, the first an elegant well-sprung travelling coach, the other slightly less grand.

'A moment more, dear Baroness,' she cried, craning forward once again to get a better view. 'We are to have company, I think. In fact . . . yes, I am almost certain that our neighbours are about to arrive! Oh, no! My handkerchief!' This last was accompanied by a muffled shriek.

Lottie felt that matters were getting out of hand. In amused exasperation, she took Sophia firmly by the arm and propelled her away from the rail.

'Enough,' she said.

'But my handkerchief . . .?'

'A mere trifle, my dear child. Josef shall send one of the servants down for it later.'

It was really nothing more than idle curiosity that persuaded Lottie to glance over the rail. The handkerchief was drifting down on the merest breath of a breeze and even as she watched, it landed at the feet of the exceedingly fashionable gentleman who at that moment stepped down from the travelling coach.

He stood with a certain indolent grace shouldering a slim walking cane, head bent in contemplation of the scrap of cambric.

Lottie ought to have withdrawn at once, but an overriding curiosity to catch a glimpse of the face of the gentleman so maddeningly hidden beneath the curling brim of the beaver hat held her motionless. At last he moved with the speed and agility of a born fencer. The cane flashed down to scoop up the handkerchief. Only when it was safe in his hand did his eyes lift to the balcony. There was a fleeting impression of well-formed classical features as he touched the handkerchief to his lips in mocking salute and made her an infinitesimal bow before turning away to assist a beautiful young woman to alight from the coach.

The whole incident had taken no more than a moment, but the effect on Lottie was out of all proportion to the passage of time. Even before she stepped back, her hands had moved instinctively to conceal the bright flags of colour flying in her cheeks. The inference conveyed in the salutation had been unmistakable. He had taken her for . . . had supposed that she had deliberately . . . No, it didn't bear thinking of! Oh, if only she had not been tempted to look down!

Princess Sophia was watching her in some curiosity and not a little puzzlement. It was so unlike Baroness Lottie to be in such a flurry. How often had she not envied the ease with which the older woman carried off situations that would have quite sunk anyone else. Sophia peered swiftly over the rail again in the hope of discovering what could have caused such a degree of discomfiture, but there was nothing to be seen except a plump lady being helped down from the carriage by a servant.

'Baroness?' She touched Lottie's arm diffidently. 'Are you all right?'

Lottie, mortified to be caught making such a cake of herself, recovered her addled wits sufficiently to exclaim, 'Yes, of course! I must have leaned a little too far, and just for a moment I felt quite strange!' She was gabbling and saw that Sophia remained unconvinced. She took a deep breath to conclude with a self-denigrating laugh, 'You see, my dear, that's what comes of behaving in an unseemly fashion!'

A tiny frown still marred Sophia's brow and her rich brown eyes were frankly considering. But before any more could be said, Fräulein Lanner's voice broke upon them, lifted in cold reprimand, exhorting Her Royal Highness to come in at once before she should be recognized. The governess had entered the room in time to witness the unnerving spectacle of her charge hanging from the balcony like a common bawd. The shock robbed her of speech. But not for long.

'I wonder that Your Highness should show so little regard for your reputation. *Gott im Himmel!* I dare not hazard what the Prince your father would say were he to learn of such conduct!'

Her thin-lipped disapproval was clearly meant to embrace the Baroness also, and as a result it affected Sophia in a quite unexpected way. A week, even a day or two earlier, such a rebuke would have crushed the young girl. Now, as she walked slowly back into the room, the royal bearing so rigorously fostered by the Fräulein was very evident. She matched the pallid flaxen-haired governess for coldness.

'Well, there is no way he *can* learn of it, is there, Fräulein? Unless you mean to inform him.'

She delivered the challenge with an hauteur so reminiscent

of her father that Lottie could have cheered.

Fräulein Lanner blanched visibly. Beneath a shapeless black bodice her inadequate bosom heaved with the force of her indignation. She opened her mouth to reply – gulped like a fish – and then closed it again as though thinking better of entering into vulgar argument.

The ornate clock on the mantelshelf chimed clear and bell-like into the lengthening silence, and Lottie, who was essentially a fair-minded young woman, felt a sudden rush of sympathy for the governess. After all, it was to some extent her own indulgence of Sophia, even, it must be confessed, a certain laxness on her part, that had contributed to the present uncomfortable atmosphere. A little generosity, therefore, would not come amiss.

'I'm sorry, Fräulein,' she said pleasantly. 'I fear I must bear much of the blame for the disruption of our routine. But there have been so many distractions – dressmakers to be accommodated, social calls that must be returned. And it is, after all, Prince Adolphus' wish that Sophia should be introduced to society.' She smiled, inviting the governess to appreciate the difficulty. 'Surely, in the circumstances, a little flexibility is allowable?'

But Fräulein Lanner showed not the slightest disposition to be generous in return. With something remarkably like a flounce, she strutted to the door, turning as she reached it to say icily, 'You know my views, Baroness. But it is clear that they carry very little weight. Perhaps you will be so good as to inform me when it will be convenient for the Princess to resume her studies.'

'Oh dear!' sighed Lottie as the door closed behind her.

'Why did you attempt to apologize to Fräulein Lanner?' Sophia demanded. 'She should not be permitted to speak to you as she did. She is little more than a servant, after all!'

Having had her peaceful overtures thrown back in her face Lottie was tempted to agree with the Princess. But as her glance rested pensively on the stiff little figure, the touch of arrogance in the youthfully rounded chin, a certain reservation made her pause. It was natural that the Bayersdorf pride should be bred in Sophia, of course, and kept under strict control, a little of it would be no bad thing – she had been timid for too long – but as for encouraging it as Fräulein Lanner did, at the expense of those gentler qualities in Sophia's nature, perhaps inherited from her mother whom Lottie had never known? A vivid picture of the child's grandmother flashed into her mind. One would not wish her to grow in that fashion!

'My dear,' she said, with only the gentlest hint of a reproof in her voice. 'You are growing up very fast, but you still have much to learn. Sometimes it is diplomatic to give a little – even with servants, and the Fräulein is rather more than that, don't you think?'

A suffusing blush betrayed the young girl's sensitivity to criticism, and a nagging uncertainty made her stammer. 'B-but in this case she was most offensive in her manner towards you!'

'Oh, my dear child, if that is all!' Lottie's laugh spilled out. 'I am not so easily offended, I assure you. If a little judicious pouring of oil can help to defuse a difficult situation, it would be foolish of me to baulk at attempting it simply because my feelings are a trifle hurt!' Reassured by the impression her words were having, she added more seriously, 'Besides, I think we should make allowances for Fräulein Lanner. She must be aware that her position with you will very soon be at an end – and I daresay it is not easy to be obliged to leave the place that has been your home for so long, knowing that you must begin all over again somewhere else.'

All the warmth so often buried beneath Sophia's shyness rushed to the surface. Her eyes kindled as she ran to take Lottie's hands. 'Oh, how wise you are! And how truly kind! I do so wish to be like you!'

It was an entirely spontaneous little speech, and as such touched Lottie deeply. But it also troubled her, not least because her true feelings concerning Fräulein Lanner were anything but charitable. Also, she had no wish to find herself the recipient of Sophia's adoration – it would be tiresome indeed to be placed on a pedestal.

So she said briskly, 'I'm not being kind at all, just practical, as I hope you will be.' And, as a slightly puzzled look came into Sophia's eyes, 'Surely you can see that it might be prudent to humour the Fräulein – just a little?'

The Princess' softly curving lower lip jutted wilfully. 'I am too old now for schooling.'

Lottie considered this pronouncement with every appearance of gravity. 'For normal schooling I agree, but I did promise your father that you would continue with your language studies, and your music – you have a great musical gift and it would be a pity were you to dissipate it for want of a little resolution.' She smiled persuasively. 'Two hours a day should suffice. Would that be such an imposition?'

The Princess was wavering and Lottie played quite shamelessly on her feelings. 'I confess it would ease my conscience, for I am only too aware that I have been shockingly neglectful of my promise to your father.' The admission had the desired effect, with Sophia eager to make amends.

Left alone, Lottie smothered her guilt with the righteous conclusion that persuasion was better than confrontation – and, less righteously, that she could ill-afford to antagonize the Fräulein more than was necessary. With any luck, she could not have witnessed the whole of what had taken place on the balcony, but nevertheless she would take a great delight in reporting this latest evidence of Lottie's light-mindedness to the Dowager Princess, whose creature she was.

Still vivid in Lottie's mind was the memory of the furore at the Schloss Bayersdorf when Prince Adolphus' plans for Sophia's projected visit to Vienna, and his purpose in sending her in the Baroness' charge first broke upon the Dowager Princess. Her wrath had been truly awesome and there were times during the days that followed when Lottie had been convinced that, by sheer force of stamina, Her Serene Highness' will must prevail. But in the event her son's stubbornness proved equal to her own, and for days an ominous atmosphere had prevailed.

Finally, and with an ill grace, the Dowager Princess had been obliged to concede defeat, although as the preparations went forward Lottie still feared that this might not be the end of the matter. Thwarted in her initial attempt to impose her will, the old lady might yet gather her strength in order to attempt the journey to Vienna, where, freed from her son's presence, she would be able to wield a much greater influence.

So far, it had not happened, but Lottie was under no

illusion. Although spared the physical presence of Her Serene Highness, her shadow still loomed over them; at every turn there would be eyes and ears observing every trifling act – not merely Fräulein Lanner, but more dangerously in the person of Countess von Deiter, whose dislike of the late Secretary of State's young widow simmered with threatening persistence beneath a surface veil of politeness. Where Prince Paul fitted into the scheme of things, Lottie wasn't sure – as yet, he had not put in an appearance. But even discounting him, the Dowager Princess would not want for informants.

However, Lottie refused to be intimidated. She had the full authority of Prince Adolphus to back her, together with his total confidence in her judgement. A niggling worry at the corner of her mind that the Prince might not have envisaged the proliferation of gaiety likely to envelop them, with all its attendant effects upon his daughter's as yet untried susceptibilities, was swiftly banished.

Sophia had lived closeted like a novice in a nunnery for long enough; if, as seemed likely, she was destined to take up the burden of responsibility for her country sooner rather than later, it was doubly important that she should be made aware of how the rest of the world went on. Besides which, Lottie was more than ever determined that the child should have a little innocent fun – something to look back on when tiresome duty held her in thrall.

When Josef presently entered the room he found the Baroness seated by the window, deep in introspection, the eyes of the little dog at her feet echoing her pensive expression.

The way of things was sometimes very strange, Josef mused. Who would now believe that when Baron Raimund had first announced that he was to marry – and not a woman of the world, but a young girl not yet dry behind the ears – all the major-domo's sensibilities had been outraged. 'To introduce such a one into a household that has been wholly masculine for more than thirty years is not to be borne,' he had railed at an equally distraught valet. 'Never in all these years has a woman resided beneath this roof! Now, it is too late for change – and such a change! I shall give notice to quit.'

But the Baron had talked him round. 'Give it six months, Josef,' he had said quietly. 'And then we shall see.' A devious man, the Baron, for long before the six months were at an end, it was as though she had always been there. And now that his beloved master had gone to his eternal reward, Josef's allegiance to the Baroness was absolute, his devotion to her as great as it had ever been to her husband.

He coughed now, discreetly.

Lottie came abruptly out of the reverie into which she had fallen – and which had concerned amongst other images that of a most elegant gentleman. Her voice was unusually crisp, businesslike.

Was the Baroness aware, Josef enquired in confidential tones that managed to convey his contempt for their present living arrangements, that they were at last possessed of neighbours? An English gentleman and two ladies – one young and very beautiful, if Hans were to be believed . . .

They exchanged a brief smile in recognition of their newest young footman's undoubted partiality for beautiful women.

'– and one older and less so,' Josef concluded.

'Let us hope they will prove congenial.' Lottie tossed the words off with deliberate nonchalance, adding the silent rider – 'and pray heaven that the gentleman is cursed with shortsightedness!' A forlorn expectation since she was obliged to admit that he would need to be blind not to know her again. However, *if* he was a gentleman . . . She became aware that Josef was proffering his small silver salver upon which reposed a lone white card, his voice still hushed, as he informed her that the said gentleman desired a few words, if she would permit.

Lottie swallowed an involuntary flutter of apprehension as she picked up the card with every appearance of composure and silently contemplated the nature of the gentleman's few words. The name, black-lettered, leapt boldly off the page at her. Maxim Annesley. It had a ring of quality – of authority, even. Guessing that he was probably just beyond the door, she allowed a significant pause to elapse before saying clearly, 'By all means, Josef. Show Mr Annesley in.'

He came with an air of calm, quiet assurance which suffered a slight reverse as their eyes met. Recognition was instantaneous, but recovery was equally swift, earning Lottie's grudging admiration.

Eyes of a clear light blue, thickly lashed, held a cool speculative gleam. 'Baroness Raimund?'

The veriest suspicion of disbelief in the clipped formality of the deep voice prompted Tasha to emerge with unaccustomed temerity from the shelter of Lottie's skirts in order to make a growling, protesting skirmish in defence of her mistress.

The piquancy of the situation, the sight of Tasha so nobly challenging this pattern card of perfection in his dove-grey inexpressibles, his coat of plain but impeccable cut, and his cravat that was a miracle of deceptive simplicity, quite restored Lottie's good humour.

Mr Annesley turned a severe gaze upon the impetuous spaniel, and with the air of one abjectly acknowledging a mistake she immediately backed away, ears drooping and apology clearly evident in her soulful eyes.

'Craven creature!' Lottie laughingly accused her erstwhile champion. 'To be so easily routed!' And then, turning to her visitor, she held out a hand, meeting his narrowed eyes with a look of amused challenge, as though prepared to call his bluff. 'Mr Annesley, how good of you to call so soon. Pray allow me to offer you some refreshment.' He declined and she nodded to Josef who quietly withdrew.

The eyes had become bright, considering slits. 'Forgive me – I had not expected. You *are* Baroness Raimund?' She inclined her head in gracious assent. 'But – you are English, surely?'

'Oh, I see! Please.' She indicated one of the many ornate sofas and disposed herself gracefully nearby, smoothing her silk skirts with unhurried ease. 'Yes. My father was Sir Charles Weston of the Foreign Office. Perhaps you knew him?'

'No, we never met, though I do have some dim recollection of his having met an unfortunate and somewhat premature end some years ago. An accident, was it not, in one of those quaint little German states?'

'Gellenstadt,' she said distinctly, resenting the faint note of disparagement in his voice. 'It is my home now. My husband was for many years Secretary of State to His Serene Highness, Grand Prince Adolphus.' She sounded pompous, and knew it – and from the way his eyebrow quirked, she knew that he thought so, too.

'He died a little over two years ago,' she added quietly.

'I'm sorry.'

He didn't sound in the least sorry to Lottie.

'Gellenstadt?' he mused. 'Isn't that the place famed for its exquisitely designed silverware? My uncle has several rather fine pieces, I believe.'

She was immediately mollified. 'Each piece is quite unique,' she explained with pride.

He nodded. 'That will be it, then. I thought the name sounded familiar. You must forgive me. My knowledge of the minor German principalities is sketchy, to say the least.'

With a cutting retort already on the tip of her tongue, Lottie hesitated. 'Drop a word in the right ear.' That was the charge Prince Adolphus had laid upon her and daunting though she found the prospect, she meant to carry it through insofar as she was able. Suppose this elegant gentleman sitting so much at his ease opposite her possessed just such an ear – or was acquainted with those who had? In fairness she had to admit that he looked exactly the kind of person who would move in the first circles, and if that were so, it might be prudent to humour him.

She schooled her features into a wry smile. 'Pray, don't apologize, Mr Annesley. I can quite appreciate that to an outsider our tiny principality must seem of scant importance, but you must surely agree that significance is not invariably determined by size. We in Gellenstadt are fiercely jealous of our independence and Prince Adolphus is determined that we shall keep it. It is his earnest hope that he will if necessary be able to count upon the support and understanding of the British delegation.'

That ought to produce some kind of reaction on his part, she decided with a certain degree of satisfaction, but unless one could account an infinitesimal movement of one eyebrow as a reaction, her judgement would seem to be quite out.

He said merely, 'Such optimism is commendable, ma'am. One can only hope that it may not prove to be ill-founded.'

'You think they won't wish to help?' she asked abruptly.

'I really haven't the slightest idea, Baroness.' His expression belied his words, indicating that he had little expectation of it, and even less opinion of women who dabbled in politics. 'It is none of my concern, thank God! But from what little I hear, representatives of the so-called great Powers have been so busily engaged in trying to carve up Europe, each to his own satisfaction, over the past few weeks, that I doubt they will have a thought to spare for more trifling matters.'

Lottie's chin came up instinctively, and try as she might she could not keep her indignation wholly in check. 'You are of course entitled to your opinion, sir, though I fear you are a cynic. Perhaps when you have been rather longer in Vienna, you will be able to judge for yourself how amiably everyone goes on.'

'Perhaps so.' But his face again wore that look of polite disbelief, and she noticed that a trace of impatience had entered his voice. 'The subtleties of politics must always fascinate, of course, but I wonder, ma'am, if I might come to the purpose of my visit?'

Drat the man! She marvelled at the ease with which he could manage to put one in the wrong.

'By all means,' she said, determined to remain pleasant though the effort choked her. 'How thoughtless of me to rattle on when you must be tired and have a thousand things to vex you after your journey. Travelling long distances can be trying at the best of times, and particularly now that the roads are so choked with people crowding into Vienna – I daresay the ladies in your party must be worn to a thread!' A sudden rush of sympathy warmed her voice. 'If there is any way I may be of service, pray do not hesitate to tell me.'

He did not answer immediately, and Lottie looked up in some surprise to see him rise and move restively to stare out of the window. Tasha uttered an obligatory bark and was instantly silenced. When Mr Annesley finally swung round, the bright sunlight behind him seemed to plane his classical features into a pattern of deep shadows.

'When I made the initial arrangements for this visit, I particularly requested that a pianoforte should be installed for my sister's use. Alys is not strong, although I am hopeful that a change of scene might prove beneficial –'

A change of company might benefit the poor girl even more, Lottie thought uncharitably. 'Well, there are certainly any number of delightful diversions to tempt Miss Annesley when she begins to feel more the thing,' she suggested.

'Alys goes about very little,' he continued repressively. 'Which is why music forms such an important part in her life. Unfortunately, my instructions would appear to have been overlooked. There is no pianoforte – and it occurred to me that there might have been some misunderstanding –'

Lottie frowned. 'Misunderstanding?'

'I believe I heard someone playing in here soon after we arrived.'

She found herself being subjected to an inquisitorial stare for all the world as though the blame for any lapse could be set squarely at her door. It took every ounce of resolution to hold on to her temper, but Lottie had not been Otto's wife for six years without learning how to cope with just such a situation. She stood up and faced him, quite unaware that the sunlight, whose shadows dealt so severely with Mr Annesley's features, had quite the opposite effect on her own, highlighting the burnished tints in her hair and the long graceful line of her jaw, lifted now in outraged dignity; most of all, it played the strangest tricks with her eyes, giving to their purple-blue depths an intense luminosity which in truth was mostly attributable to anger.

'If you mean *do we have your pianoforte*, Mr Annesley, then no, we do not. The young lady you heard playing is the Crown Princess Sophia of Gellenstadt who is presently in my care. The Princess is also a highly gifted musician. Her father was most anxious that she should not fall behind with her tuition during her stay in Vienna and took the appropriate steps to ensure that she would not.'

Mr Annesley's jaw tightened perceptibly, affording Lottie a curious satisfaction. It prompted her to add magnanimously, 'However, your sister is very welcome to come and practice here whenever she pleases. It is but a step across the hallway, after all.'

It was difficult to interpret the expression that flickered across his face for it was gone in a moment and he was saying stiffly, 'Thank you – but that will not be at all convenient.'

'I'm sorry you feel that way. Perhaps if you were to ask your sister she might feel better disposed towards the idea.'

Challengingly their eyes locked – and neither, it seemed, was disposed to give way.

Heavens! What a ridiculous situation, thought Lottie, suddenly seeing the funny side. Two full-grown adults who should know better, standing here brangling over so trifling a matter.

'Oh look,' she exclaimed impulsively, her mouth curving into a spontaneous smile. 'This is all quite absurd! I am truly sorry about your sister's pianoforte – of course you must procure one for her, and indeed there must be any number of excellent instruments to be had in a city like Vienna if one did but know where to look for them! How would it be if my major-domo, Josef, who has many friends here, were to make a few inquiries for you?'

But Mr Annesley declined to grasp the olive branch. He thanked her again for her kind offices, implied that he was not without connections himself, and expressed the conviction that he would be able to contrive something.

'Fine. Then there is little more to be said.' Lottie stepped across the room and gave the bellrope a sharp tug. Hardly was the gesture complete however, when to her astonishment the door opened to admit Prince Paul. He crossed the room with the lithe grace that was so much a part of him – handsome as ever, his uniform glittering with silver braid, his eyes full of laughing demons – while in the doorway behind him, Josef lifted his shoulders at the Baroness in a fatalistic shrug.

Paul greeted Lottie with lazy familiarity, gave an unconvincingly exaggerated start upon seeing that she was not alone, and came forward to take her hands in his and kiss her lightly on both cheeks.

'Allow me to tell you how delightful you are looking, my dear.' Ever sensitive to atmosphere, he glanced with interest from her to Mr Annesley and back again. 'A thousand pardons if I intrude,' he said with mock humility, 'but families seldom stand on ceremony, and we are *almost* family, are we not?'

Lottie's patience was by now sorely tried. She said more sharply than she had intended, 'Certainly not, Highness!' and could hardly fail to be aware of the way his eyes widened. Reluctantly she introduced the two men, explaining pointedly that Mr Annesley had that very day arrived to take up residence in the adjoining apartment, and had but called to pay his respects.

'Very civil of you, sir. It was my intention, also.'

Prince Paul was charm itself, Mr Annesley scrupulously correct as they exchanged politenesses – and Lottie wished them both at the devil.

'We must not keep Mr Annesley, your Highness,' she interposed at last with a dexterity that brought a gleam of appreciation to both pairs of eyes. 'I am sure that he will be wishing to get back to his sister.' She turned to him. 'Do give Miss Annesley my very kindest regards. Perhaps we shall be able to meet when she is feeling more the thing.'

'No doubt you will.' He said it without enthusiasm, seemed on the point of saying more, and then, with a frowning glance in Prince Paul's direction, bowed and walked swiftly to the door. There, to Lottie's surprise, he hesitated, then turned and retraced his steps. Looking her full in the eyes, he felt in his pocket and withdrew an all too familiar scrap of cambric, lavishly embellished with the Gellenstadt crest. 'This is your property, I believe?'

She opened her mouth to deny it, thought better of it – and blushed most betrayingly as he pressed it into her hand.

'Quite so. I was sure you would recognize it. One of your maidservants tossed it to me from the balcony as I was arriving earlier. An exceedingly pert young baggage –' he paused to observe the effect of his words with some relish before concluding softly, 'I trust she will be severely reprimanded for her forwardness.'

It was not often that Lottie found herself bereft of words, but when Josef had closed the door behind Mr Annesley she was still standing, clutching the handkerchief, unaware that Prince Paul was watching her intently until he addressed her in his most satirical manner.

'Well, well, lovely Lottie! What a highly diverting little charade that was! Is one permitted to enquire what it was all about?

What indeed? She was not entirely sure herself, though she rather suspected that Mr Annesley had been laughing at her. She uttered a vexatious little exclamation and turned to meet Prince Paul's mocking glance with what self-possession she could muster.

'A trifling incident, 'Highness – hardly worth repeating,' she said, tucking the handkerchief casually into her sleeve. And then, swiftly, before he could persist, she changed the subject. 'Have you been long in Vienna? For I'm bound to say we have seen nothing of you?'

His amused inclination of the head left her wondering whether he was acceding to her wishes or saluting her *sang-froid*, but whatever the reason, it did little to soothe her already exacerbated nerves.

'Would that I could convince myself that you had looked for me,' he murmured provocatively. 'In fact, I have been with Franz von Gratz. He has a rather pleasant shooting lodge in the Bavarian mountains. You have met Duke Franz, I think?'

Lottie had indeed. He had visited the Schloss several years ago, and it was a measure of the impression he had made that Lottie remembered him still, for he had reminded her irresistibly of an eagle – a high forehead, deep-set, hooded eyes, and a bold nose above a brutal chin – an ambitious man who, like Prince Paul, craved power. There was no denying that he was both imposing and gallant, but always she had sensed a hint of danger behind the affability. Prince Adolphus did not like him at all.

'We arrived in Vienna this morning,' Paul continued, 'and as you see, I could not wait to present myself to you.'

A terrible thought crossed Lottie's mind. 'You don't . . . that is to say, you do have your accommodation arranged?'

He grinned lazily. 'And if I had not? Would you find me a bed?' There was an infinitesimal silence during which she strove to hide her disquiet, but from the way his grin widened it was clear that he had read her mind with embarrassing accuracy. 'I have often remarked that you do have the most eloquent eyes, dear Baroness! But fear not. Franz has a charming house in Am Hof. I come merely to pay my respects to my niece and her delightful chaperone – and to offer you my humble services as escort to the Grand Rout at the Palace next week. You mean to go, of course?'

'Yes,' Lottie prevaricated, 'but Sophia is not yet Out, so she is not invited.'

'I had not supposed that she would be,' he said smoothly. 'Shall we take that as arranged then? And perhaps before that, you will give me the pleasure of taking you and Sophia to the opera one evening?'

As she murmured reluctant agreement, Lottie told herself that it was all perfectly innocent, this desire of his to please. So why did she have the oddest feeling that there was more to it than appeared on the surface?

2

The door on the other side of the landing stood open when Lottie, with Tasha at her heels, stepped out on the following morning to make a few purchases. She hesitated at the head of the staircase, uncertain whether or not to risk a rebuff by walking across to ask after Miss Annesley's health, and chiding herself for being so poor-spirited as to care if she were snubbed.

While she was still pondering the matter, there came a clatter of feet above her and the sound of voices. Two young men in the oddest, brightest assortment of clothing came into view. They paused to eye her with a healthy interest, swept her an exaggeratedly gallant bow before, with an ebullient '*Guten Morgen, Fräulein*,' they ran on down the stairs, their happy laughter echoing back, then fading.

In some curious way their carefree passing swept away all of Lottie's reservations; she was still smiling as she reached the door to find a young footman in the act of closing it.

Totally disarmed by the Baroness' friendly manner, to say nothing of a pair of brilliant blue eyes that gave him the oddest feeling that he was drowning, he stammered slightly as he explained that Mr Annesley had gone out a few minutes earlier, but yes, of course he would enquire if Miss Annesley or her companion Mrs Osmond were receiving.

Lottie was shown into a small anteroom, elegantly and extravagantly appointed. She was soon lost in contemplation of a lacquered cabinet on a stand of wood, elaborately carved and covered with beaten silver; effective, she thought, but the workmanship lacked the intricate delicacy of Gellenstadt silverware.

Behind her a soft musical voice said, 'Baroness Raimund? How very kind of you to call,' and she turned to find the breath catching in her throat.

Miss Annesley, for it must be she, stood quietly near the door, a wand-slim, fragile-looking girl in a simple high-waisted white muslin dress. Angelic seemed too trite a word to describe her, yet was there not a heart-stopping quality of otherworldliness in the sweet symmetry of her features – her creamy translucent skin framed by soft caught-back hair, more silver than gold, and her wide gentle eyes a clear light grey?

Lottie realized that she was staring, and quickly pulled herself together.

'You must think me very rude,' she said, advancing with outstretched hand. 'But you are not at all what I was expecting.' She laughed. 'Oh dear, that sounds almost as bad! What I mean is, you are not very like your brother, are you?'

The answering gurgle of laughter was vibrant with affection. 'I suppose not. But then, there is no one quite like Max!'

Lottie was stupidly slow to answer, as dismay held her tongue cleaved to the roof of her mouth. Her arm fell back.

Alys Annesley said quietly into the silence, 'You didn't know. I had supposed Max must have told you that I am blind.'

'No.' The single word was scarcely audible.

'Then it must have come as a nasty shock. But you mustn't feel awkward, or sorry for me, you know. I am really very fortunate.'

Fortunate! Lottie stared at her, but there was no trace of irony and certainly no self-pity in the soft voice. Why, oh why, had Mr Annesley not said something – anything! Then she would not have made such a fool of herself!

'I wonder . . . would you mind, Baroness?' For the first time a note of uncertainty entered Miss Annesley's voice. She held out her own hand with a nervous little laugh. 'At home I am quite independent, but I don't know my way round here yet . . .'

Lottie quickly took the outstretched fingers in a firm reassuring clasp and guided the girl to a sofa. When they were both seated, she asked with some diffidence, 'Have you always been . . .'

'Blind? Please, you must not be afraid to say it.' The voice was steadily matter-of-fact. 'It happened four years ago – a riding accident when I was just sixteen.' A hint of wistfulness was ruthlessly suppressed. 'I was something of a harum-scarum in those days, and got my just deserts when I took a toss over a fence when I shouldn't have been out at all. It was horrid for a while, but sooner or later one must come to terms if one's life is not to be wholly blighted – and friends were so good. Max was marvellous – without him I might well have gone under!'

Was there a defensive note in her voice, Lottie wondered? If so, it was gone in a moment.

'I seldom leave home in the ordinary way, so everything seems a little strange to me still. But Max wished to attend the Congress and he thought that it might be an agreeable change for me to visit Vienna.'

This did not quite accord with what Mr Annesley had told Lottie. What had he said of the Congress? 'It is no concern of mine, thank God!' She chided herself for being unwarrantably suspicious. It was probably no more than his way of warding off what he thought of as petticoat politics.

Tasha meanwhile had been drawn by the soft voice to investigate the slim hand resting on the sofa nearest to her. As the damp nose touched her skin, Alys' fingers turned instinctively to tickle her gently under the chin before moving upwards to find that very particular spot beneath the ear that only the true dog-lover knows about. Tasha uttered a soft, blissful whine and leaned in to the sensitive fingers.

'Oh, you have your little dog with you – a spaniel, is she not?' Alys fondled Tasha's ears until she squirmed with delight. 'I have two retrievers at home and I do miss them most dreadfully. They take me for walks, and I always feel quite safe with them.'

Again Lottie heard that hint of wistfulness. 'Well, I am quite willing to share Tasha with you,' she said lightly. 'She is usually rather timid, but I can see that you have made a conquest!'

'Do you think so? Cousin Carrie – Mrs Osmond, that is – usually acts as my eyes when Max is not about, but she is in her room writing letters, so I asked Morgan, our young footman, to bring me to you as I did so want to meet you –' She stopped on a rueful breathless little laugh. 'Oh dear, I am chattering too much! I always do when I am nervous.'

'Nonsense, my dear,' Lottie reassured her. 'And talking is

my besetting sin, so I am quite an authority!'

'Yes, Max said that you –' Miss Annesley stopped, biting her lip.

'I can imagine what your brother said,' came the amused reply. 'Frivolous, argumentative – and altogether too opinionated for a woman!'

'Oh, no, Baroness! That is . . .' An embarrassed damask blush stole over the lovely face. 'He *did* say that you have very definite ideas.'

Lottie laughed. 'Well, I've had far worse things said about me, my dear Miss Annesley, so pray don't let it trouble you.'

'Oh, please,' said the girl shyly, 'will you not call me Alys? Miss Annesley sounds so formal and I would so like us to be friends!'

'My dear, nothing would please me more, so long as you will call me Lottie in return. Baroness sounds even more forbidding, don't you think?'

'I must say it did sound a bit daunting at first – a baroness and a *princess* living next door – but I got Max to describe you in minute detail.' Lottie found herself wishing that she could have been privy to *that* conversation. 'Also, it was clear from Morgan's voice just now, when he spoke your name, that he was already enslaved!'

'Heavens!'

'You can tell a great deal from voices, you know,' Alys continued gravely. 'Yours is so bubbly and friendly that I feel as though I have known you for ever.'

'Well, as soon as we can arrange it, you must come and meet Princess Sophia. She is very sweet and unspoiled – and not in the least daunting! She will be delighted to meet someone young, especially someone who shares her love of music.' Lottie remembered the pianoforte, and in spite of Mr Annesley's rejection of her offer, she again made it.

'Oh, I should like that very much,' said Alys enthusiastically. 'Max is hoping to have our own instrument installed quite soon, but it would be such fun to share with someone meanwhile.'

'Good. That is decided then. Who knows, you might become accomplished duettists.' It gave Lottie an unconscionable glow of satisfaction to visualise Mr Annesley's wrath upon discovering that his wishes had been circumvented.

As it happened they were destined to meet that same evening at the opera house. Lottie had returned from her shopping rather later than she had intended to find Prince Paul stretched out in a chair before the fire, looking very much at home, with Sophia settled on a stool at his feet.

'What a very homely picture!' she said, betraying asperity in the way she stripped off her gloves and tossed them on to a side table near the door. Her eyes met Prince Paul's.

'Quite avuncular, in fact,' he agreed innocently. 'I am fast discovering the joys of family that I have ignored for so long.'

Sophia turned a shining face up to Lottie. 'Uncle Paul has come to invite us to the opera tonight. There is to be a ballet called *Flore and Zephire*. Do say that we can go, *dear* Baroness Lottie! The dancer is a very famous lady, Signora . . .' she looked questioningly at the Prince.

'Bitottini,' he supplied, his mouth quirking into a mocking smile. 'May I echo Sophia's plea? Do say that you will come, *dear* Baroness Lottie?'

With nothing more definite in prospect than the usual round of assemblies, to none of which she was definitely promised, there was no way she could refuse without appearing downright mean-spirited, and well he knew it. Yet it troubled Lottie to observe the ease with which he had conquered the shy niece who had until recently regarded him with distant awe, and whom he in turn had scarcely deigned to notice at all.

Now, in the space of a day, Sophia was already blossoming in the warmth of his regard, and he had charmed her as only he could into believing that, in the unfortunate absence of her father, he considered it to be his bounden duty to see her launched into society as a Bayersdorf should be. And Lottie could not rid herself of the suspicion that Paul seldom did anything without a reason.

However, having agreed to the visit, she was determined that he should have no fault to find with their appearance. When he arrived that evening he found his niece in white spangled gauze, demurely fashioned, with tiny puffed sleeves and ribbons floating from a simple high waist. Sophia was as ethereally lovely as only a girl of seventeen could be.

Prince Paul held her away from him, his expert eye noting

with approval the silver ribbons that Lottie's own maid, Gertrude, had threaded among her gleaming dark curls.

'Excellent,' he said as she twirled for his benefit. 'The young men are to be envied, *Liebchen!*' He patted her cheek and turned his attention to her chaperone. 'I congratulate you, my dear Baroness. But then, your taste was ever impeccable.'

'You are too kind,' she said, only too aware that he was subjecting her to a similar scrutiny. 'But shouldn't we be on our way, if we are not to be late?'

His look grew quizzical. 'If you say so, Baroness.' But there was a familiarity in his manner that irritated her. She was aware of it even in the dim confines of the coach as it made its way through the jostling streets; as he returned lazy answers to Sophia's shy eager questions, the flambeaux and lanterns of other coaches crisscrossing their path caught the glint of his eyes watching her, and instinctively she was put on her mettle.

In the foyer of the opera house she moved with a confident grace, looking precisely what she was – a fashionable young matron, well able to hold her own amid the glittering throng, her slim figure shown to advantage in a gown of deep blue twilled silk. The bodice was cut in the Austrian style, a gauze shawl draped her elbows and a frivolous little cap adorned her upswept hair, and to complete the picture, she wore the sapphires that had been Otto's wedding gift to her.

'Quite exquisite,' murmured Prince Paul. 'It is more than time that you abandoned your self-imposed incarceration in Gellenstadt and rejoined the human race!'

'I haven't abandoned anything,' she retorted with spirit. 'I enjoy my life at home. This is but a holiday.'

He laughed softly. 'So you say, lovely Lottie. So you say.'

She turned away from him in exasperation, and Mr Annesley, standing no more than a few feet away unexpectedly received the full scorching intensity of her blazing blue eyes, which widened perceptibly upon meeting his faintly amused, if perplexed ones. He inclined his head, and with an oddly distrait gesture she turned her back on him and was almost immediately laughing and talking with several people who had strolled up to join her party – among them a dashing young colonel of the Czar's Imperial Guard, and a large aggressively handsome figure that Mr Annesley instinctively labelled 'Teutonic nobility.'

From their reactions it was soon apparent that Baroness Raimund's air of gaiety was infectious. Even at this distance, he was aware of her warm vitality; saw how, with every graceful movement, her silk gown shimmered in the light, rippling down the length of her body in a way that was unconsciously revealing. Involuntarily he was reminded of his first tantalizing glimpse of her as she had dropped the handkerchief at his feet, and a fleeting smile kindled his eyes.

The statuesque lady at his side had witnessed the intriguing little charade and was eager to know more.

'Who *is* that exceedingly striking young woman, Max?' she demanded in her usual forthright way. 'There is something about her . . . I feel almost sure that I must have met her at some time.'

'I shouldn't think that at all likely,' he said dryly. 'Unless you are familiar with a place called Gellenstadt. Baroness Raimund is the somewhat unlikely relict of that principality's former Secretary of State. You may, however, have been acquainted with her late father, who for many years enjoyed a rather successful roving commission with our own foreign ministry until his untimely death. Sir Charles Weston?'

'Gracious goodness!' Lady Merrivale exclaimed. 'Never tell me that beautiful creature is little Charlotte Weston! Why, her mother was one of my dearest friends . . .' She put up her lorgnette. 'I haven't laid eyes on Lottie since . . . oh, many years. She was somewhere about the age my Cassie is now, a big lively girl . . . apple of her father's eye, God rest him. He took her everywhere with him after her mama died. But never would I have thought she'd turn out a beauty! Max, you must take me across to her at once.'

Lottie, disconcerted by the unexpected appearance of Mr Annesley, took but a moment to assure herself that Alys was not with him, reasoned that there was nothing remarkable in his presence (and indeed, why should there be?) and returned her attention to those about her. She was soon fully occupied in guiding Sophia's still shy stumbling ventures amid the pitfalls of social conversation as, under the mocking eyes of Prince Paul, she resolutely and with admirable skill diverted all attempts by Prince Metlin to draw her young charge away from the rest. Duke Franz was less easy to cope with, for whilst he paid polite compliments to Sophia, his real interest was quite blatantly focused upon herself.

So great was her concentration that when she heard Mr Annesley's voice addressing her, the emotion uppermost in her breast was mild annoyance. Then her gaze moved to the purple-clad matron at his side and at once her face lit up.

'Lady Merrivale! Oh, what a lovely surprise!' She leaned forward to kiss the rouged cheek. 'Why, it must be all of ten years since we last met.'

Lady Merrivale's twinkling eyes were frankly appraising. 'We have both changed considerably since then – and in you, my dear, if you will permit an old friend to speak freely, the transformation is little short of miraculous!'

This was bluntness indeed. But rather to Mr Annesley's surprise, it provoked nothing from the Baroness but a trill of laughter. 'So I should hope,' she chuckled. 'Such an ungainly child as I was! But you, dear ma'am, have scarcely altered at all. Oh, how good it is to see you again like this!'

The next few minutes were taken up with introductions, in the course of which Lottie presently found herself in Mr Annesley's company.

'You called on my sister this morning, I believe?'

He was courtesy itself, and she, all too aware of having acted precipitately, was a little on the defensive. 'Yes, I did. Do you mind?'

He parried the challenging edge to her voice with an ironical lift of the brow. 'Certainly not. Why ever should you think it?'

'No reason, except . . .' Drat him, why should he make her feel guilty without due cause? Her eyes held steadfastly to his. 'Why did you not tell me . . . about your sister's blindness, I mean?'

A faint shadow passed across his face, but it was gone so swiftly that she was left wondering if she had imagined it.

'In other circumstances I should have done so.' His gaze rested momentarily on Prince Paul who in turn had his eye-glass trained upon a voluptuous brunette nearby. 'But we were interrupted,' he concluded blandly. 'And I could hardly know that you were destined to meet her so soon.'

'Pushing my way in, uninvited?' she suggested flippantly, and immediately cursed her impetuous tongue. 'No, no, forgive me, Mr Annesley! That was a monstrously unhandsome thing to say! I'm sure that no such thought was ever in your head.'

'No, it wasn't,' he admitted so gravely that she wondered if he could be quizzing her. 'I merely wished to thank you for the pleasure your visit gave to Alys.'

She bit her lip. 'Oh dear. Coals of fire, sir?'

Something remarkably like a boyish grin illuminated his face. 'Now that really *would* be unhandsome!' Her answering grin encouraged him to say, 'Baroness – do you think we might perhaps declare a truce? In view of our rather curious living arrangements, I suspect that to be for ever coming to points would soon prove exceedingly tiresome. More importantly, it would displease Alys.'

Lottie was immediately in charity with him. 'Then a truce it must be,' she exclaimed, 'for I like your sister very well, and hope that we shall soon be firm friends. She is not with you this evening?'

'No. Alys is not wholly at ease in crowded places.'

She had not been mistaken. It was there again, that indefinable something in his voice when speaking of his sister. She was intrigued and longed to know more but, unwilling to upset their new harmonious relationship, she for once schooled her impetuous tongue, saying only, 'A pity. She would so enjoy the music.'

He agreed, noncommittally, and a moment later, so smoothly that she was not sure how it had come about, Lottie found herself talking to Lady Merrivale whilst he set himself to entertain Sophia in a way that soon put her at her ease. Her ladyship's enthusiasm soon claimed Lottie's attention, leaving her no time to ponder the matter.

'My dear child, I am quite impatient to hear all that has befallen you in the past few years. Naturally one has heard rumours from time to time – such extraordinary stories that one hardly knew what to believe. You must come along and visit me very soon. We are in Ball Gasse. Bring your little princess if you think she would care for it. Merrivale ain't with us, but I have both the girls to bear me company. Arabella . . .

you'll remember Arabella, I daresay, though she was a little younger than you . . .'

Lottie dimly recalled a dark-haired child with glossy ringlets. 'She isn't with you tonight?'

'No. A migraine. Such a pity. She and Max Annesley are . . .' Her ladyship's voice sank to a confidential whisper tinged with a certain complacence. 'Well, nothing is settled, you understand, but I have every reason to hope . . . it would be such a very fine match! And then there is Cassie, my youngest daughter. She's not Out yet, not for another twelvemonth, and who is to say what might not have happened by then? Still, that is for the future. Now, you won't forget, will you?'

The glittering throng began to surge towards the auditorium and Lady Merrivale patted Lottie's hand. 'Just as soon as you have a moment to spare. Max has our direction . . . in fact, I've a mind to ask him to bring you to me.' Lottie quickly protested that this was not at all necessary. 'As you please, my dear. One forgets how used you must be to ordering your own affairs. It was only with his telling me that you are sharing neighbouring apartments. Vienna is *so* crowded, is it not? And so full of handsome young men,' she added coyly, allowing her glance to stray towards Prince Paul and his friends.

Lottie laughingly disclaimed any interest in *that* direction. 'It is Sophia who is the attraction,' she insisted, but her ladyship was not convinced.

'Nonsense,' she exclaimed, ever forthright. 'Oh, the child is a taking enough little thing, I grant you . . . very prettily behaved, too, and I don't doubt the gentlemen find her quite enchanting. But they don't look at her as they look at you!'

A telltale warmth stole into Lottie's cheeks. Prince Paul's recent behaviour had been unsettling to say the least, and her ears were still echoing with the fulsome compliments of von Gratz. 'I must go and rescue Princess Sophia,' she said in a rush of relief as she saw how all the gentlemen were beginning to cluster round her. 'The poor child will be quite overwhelmed!'

'Just so,' said Lady Merrivale dryly.

Sophia, far from being overwhelmed, however, greeted Lottie with a kind of breathless eagerness.

'Prince Metlin has been telling me how delightful it is to drive up into the Wienerwald, and how he would very much like to arrange a picnic for us there was soon as possible!'

Oh dear! Lottie sighed and gave the Prince a quizzical, half-reproachful look before saying in a bright practical voice, 'It is most kind of His Highness, but surely it's rather too late in the year to be thinking of woodland picnics?'

Prince Metlin's crooked yet oddly attractive face was alight with rueful laughter. 'Oh come, my dear Baroness – you would not be so cruel as to forbid my harmless little excursion? I envisage a very modest luncheon party – about eight to ten people, only – with plenty of rugs to ensure that no one takes a chill. Quite unexceptional, I promise you.'

As her own mouth curved reluctantly in response, Lottie found that she was no more proof against the puckish appeal of his lively amber eyes than Sophia.

'Well, we shall see,' she said.

It was with mixed feelings that she presently saw him take his leave, though she was far from pleased to discover that von Gratz was to share their box. He was punctiliously courteous and could turn a compliment as well as any man, yet he still made her feel uncomfortable, and she knew that Sophia was totally overawed by him. She couldn't help wondering whether Prince Paul had an ulterior motive for inviting him, but when she glanced his way, he returned her questioning frown with a bland smile.

Fortunately, the spellbinding romance being enacted upon the stage affected Sophia so powerfully that it totally supplanted reality, and by the end of the evening she was scarcely aware of the Duke's leavetaking. There was a dazed look in her eyes that lasted throughout the journey home, and when they arrived she had to be prompted to make her thanks to her uncle.

'One forgets that there was ever anything so young!' Prince Paul murmured as she floated dreamily away to her bed. 'It is almost a pity that such innocence cannot last.'

There was an off-handedness in the calm assumption that moved Lottie to say sharply, 'Well, for my part, I mean to ensure that Sophia keeps hers for as long as possible!'

'Do you, indeed?' He set down the glass of brandy to which he had liberally helped himself on their return, and came towards her. Not for the first time she wished there had been some way of preventing him from coming in with them, but she could hardly have had Josef bar the door to him.

Abruptly she turned away, but this was a mistake, for he clearly saw it as a challenge. He came up close behind her, his breath warm against her skin as his lips brushed her bare shoulder. A tremor rippled along her nerve ends.

'And what of your own innocence, lovely Lottie?'

It was his soft mocking laugh that spurred her to move swiftly out of his reach before turning to face him.

'With respect, Highness, the hour is late and you should not be here. I think you should leave – at once.'

He laughed again, with genuine amusement this time. 'My dear girl, we are not in Gellenstadt now, so you can drop the formality.' In a few quick strides he had crossed the room, and had encircled her wrists – not tightly, but quite inescapably. 'It really is time we got better acquainted.'

Lottie's heart was thudding, though whether from apprehension or simply rage, she couldn't be sure. But this was Paul at his most unpredictable and she had no wish to provoke him.

'Please – let me go,' she said quietly.

For answer his fingers tightened, forcing her hands behind her back and drawing her very close so that they stood, breast to breast.

'You haven't answered my question,' he murmured against her hair.

'No – because it was silly and not a little impertinent, and, as such, was better ignored,' she said, disturbed to find herself short of breath, and – yes, she had to admit it, just a little afraid. 'Now, will you please let me go?' she reiterated firmly, so that he should not guess how she felt.

'All in good time, *Lielbling*. Why did you think it impertinent, I wonder? Did I perhaps strike a little too close to home?' His face was very close, so close that the duelling scar stood out lividly, and his narrowed eyes raking her face betrayed no hint of pity in their glittering depths. 'I'll tell you what I think. I think that Otto Raimund took an unfledged girl and turned her into a woman of style and poise, a warm and generous partner, well schooled in all the social graces. In his own way, I think he even grew to love her, but . . .'

'Be silent!' she cried, incensed beyond reason. She struggled to free his hold on her, but his fingers tightened, and frustrated by her inability to strike at him physically, she took refuge in words. 'You arc insulting beyond belief, and I will not listen!'

Prince Paul's mouth quirked mockingly. 'What *will* you do – scream for Josef? I don't advise it, my dear. Such an embarrassing clash of loyalties for him!' There was a hardness beneath the sarcasm that convinced her that he would not hesitate to use his rank, should she place him in such a position. 'Besides, of what do I stand accused? I would hardly be so foolish as to attempt to prove my suspicions here where we might be interrupted. I'll not deny that I have wanted you for a very long time, and never more so than now.' He enjoyed watching the wild colour flood her face. 'But your virtue is not in any immediate danger,' and suddenly the laughing devils were in his eyes. 'Except – perhaps a kiss?'

'Why not?' She glared back at him, pouring all the scorn she could manage into her shaking voice. 'It is no more than one would expect of you – to take by force what you cannot freely earn!'

'Then I had better not disappoint you!'

Lottie had expected no quarter, but his mouth, though questing, explored hers slowly, and with a gentle expertise that made her feel very strange. At last he raised his head – and released her without a word. She covered her mouth with a trembling hand, staring at him in the continuing silence as he picked up his hat and cane.

'It is as I thought,' he said enigmatically, looking down at her with a queer triumphant little smile. And then he bowed and went quickly from the room.

Surely, Lottie reasoned, her thoughts tumbling in disarray, there was no way he could know . . . that not only had Otto never made her his wife in more than name, but more shaming still, that never until a moment ago had anyone kissed her as though she were a . . . her mind boggled over the most adequate description . . . a desirable woman!

Her legs had grown suddenly weak, and she sat down rather hurriedly, wondering if she would ever begin to understand Paul, and quite illogically hating him for arousing in her a need she had never before experienced!

3

Prince Adolphus sat severely erect in his favourite armchair close to the fire, unable, even in the privacy of his own rooms, to succumb to the rigours of physical discomfort. Every so often a scurry of hail buffeted the window, borne on the wind that had rushed down unimpeded through the mountain passes to meet its first obstacle in the high impenetrable walls of the Schloss. It soughed now beneath the eaves and round the chimneys, sending spiteful little gusts of black smoke into every room in a restive determination to gain admittance. In Prince Adolphus' room the logs in the hearth, as though affected by the general mood, settled uneasily, sending up showers of sparks to mingle with the fitful flames, flames that seemed powerless to penetrate the chill that was in his bones, so that the long slim fingers grasping the letter were faintly tinged with blue.

The missive already showed evidence of having been much read, and as he smoothed the paper yet again it required no more than the merest flight of fancy to hear the lilt of Charlotte's voice. The words were by now so familiar to him that he could have shut his eyes and recited them by heart.

Dear sire,

We are now quite settled here – and the pleasures at which I hinted when last I wrote are fast gathering pace. There is so much to tell that I scarce know where to begin. The chief protagonists are now assembled, and oh, what a merry time we have enjoyed observing the preliminaries! Would that you could be with us to share our innocent pleasures!

Czar Alexander's arrival in Vienna, dutifully accompanied by the King of Prussia, has been quite the most entertaining spectacle to date – reaching at times the dizzy heights of theatricality! They had the honour of being met by Emperor Francis, who rode out to greet them on the bank of the Danube. Then all three entered the city together, flanked by guards of honour, at the head of a procession comprising the most colourful array of princes of the blood and generals from all parts of Europe that one could ever hope to see – and to the accompaniment of church bells and cannon, and people cheering them every step of the way. As if this were not enough, the whole procedure was gone through again on the following day for the arrival of the Empress of Russia's carriage. She was accorded the added distinction of being met at the gates of the Hofburg by a group of young girls all in white, bearing baskets of flowers. I beg you will forgive my irreverence, sire, but it was all rather like a medieval pageant. Speaking of which, we are to be treated to just such an entertainment next month, with knights jousting for ladies' favours and everything!

I do wish you could see how Sophia has come on – she is excellently received everywhere, and is blossoming daily and making many young friends, not to mention attracting several beaux, none of whom need yet be taken seriously. You may be sure that I shall take the greatest pains to guard against any unwelcome attentions in that direction! Of course, she has not as yet attended any of the formal balls or assemblies, but it is my intention to hold a Coming Out ball for her very shortly – a début that will surely be the envy of any young girl, with a guest list including representatives of almost every royal family in Europe, and many other persons of influence besides. This house has the most beautiful ballroom imaginable – exactly right for such an occasion. It lies between the two apartments on the first floor and our neighbours, a Mr Annesley and his sister – English and quite agreeable – have no objection to its being used for this purpose.

Oh, by the way, your brother has recently arrived in Vienna with his friend, von Gratz. Also, Count and Countess von Deiter – strange how the latter can make me feel the weight of her disapproval, even when she is at her most charming! I am in bad grace at present over the matter of the small comfit dish which you had fashioned for the Emperor. I took it to the Hofburg myself and was graciously granted audience.

Emperor Francis was kindness itself. He was much taken with the originality of the design and gave me all kinds of messages for you, though doubtless he will be writing personally to express his pleasure. However, Count von Deiter was clearly of the opinion that I had usurped his position, and if I am honest, I must admit he has a point. Oh, well!

Here Prince Adolphus paused, the letter fluttering to his knee as he contemplated the combination of Paul and von Gratz.

Had Charlotte told him for a reason, or was he being unduly sensitive? He shrugged the thought away and read on.

With regard to less frivolous matters, very little of importance goes forward at present. Monsieur Talleyrand, with the support of Spain's Don Labrador, has raised objections to the format of the agenda already agreed by the four main Powers, as it gives him no say on territorial issues, so all is now in disarray. And no sooner had France and Spain been accommodated than Sweden and Portugal protested on similar grounds, so – heigh ho, the Big Four have now grown to Eight, and who knows where it will end?

The formal business of the Congress has been put back to the beginning of November, but there is no lack of informal discussion and speculation – no social gathering is complete without its gossiping huddle of diplomats, official and unofficial. Did I tell you that the Emperor is quite obsessed with the possible infiltration of spies among the delegations – and that he has ordered the head of his secret police, Baron Hager, to place his own spies in all the embassies and report to him each morning with their findings?

Most of our neighbouring states are excellently represented here and will, I'm sure, be jealously looking to secure their (and hopefully, our) boundaries. Only the poor King of Saxony is barred – I fear he will have to pay dearly for his involvement with Napoleon! Lord and Lady Castlereagh have shown great kindness to me – his lordship and Papa were great friends, you know – and you may be sure that I shall use any influence I might be able to command in *that* quarter!

Meanwhile Prince Metternich has been charged by the Emperor with the task of keeping us amused. He is determined that we shall not grow dull, and is arranging so many diversions for our every waking moment that I pray we shall not grow satiated with the sheer gaiety of it all!

I will write again very soon, and remain as ever, your devoted and obedient Charlotte.

Oh, I forgot to tell you – your daughter is not alone in being courted. My Tasha has also acquired an admirer – a disreputable hound of exceedingly doubtful lineage, though I'm bound to confess that what he lacks in breeding, he more than makes up for in persistence!

This brought a faint smile which slowly faded as Prince Adolphus read again that which moved him most deeply – *your devoted and obedient Charlotte*. Her departure from Gellenstadt had been like the passing of summer, for with her had gone that particular life-giving warmth that was so much a part of her. Now, for a fleeting moment, the magic returned and he could cherish the illusion that she was here with him. He drew a thick woollen shawl around his shoulders and stared unseeingly into the leaping flames.

His manservant, Carl, coming into the room unobserved, could not but be aware of a growing frailty in the Prince's condition. With the onset of winter there had come a pinched look to his face, a disturbing increase in the bouts of coughing, that moved Carl sometimes to wonder if his master would live to see another spring. But all this he kept in his heart as he moved to the Prince's side.

'Highness,' he said, touching the unmoving figure with a tentative hand. 'Her Serene Highness, your mother, is wishful to speak with you.'

Prince Adolphus roused, nodded without enthusiasm and drew the shawl closer about him as though to shield himself.

By the time his mother reached his side, there was no sign of Charlotte's letter, the only correspondence on the table beside him being a duty note from Sophia and a rambling prosy account from Count von Deiter of events already conveyed by Charlotte with such sparkling brevity.

'Good morning, Adolphus.' A dry kiss brushed his unresponsive cheek as the old lady passed him to seat herself on the formal upright chair facing him, her outstretched hands rigidly supported by her stick. 'You do not look at all well. I sometimes wonder if Mendel knows what he's about. Perhaps you should seek another opinion.'

'Thank you, Mother,' said the Prince dryly. 'But I have had my fill of doctors. Mendel will do as well as any other for my purposes.'

'As you please. I am aware that my opinion counts for very little here.' Her glance darted with reptilian swiftness towards the table at his elbow. 'You have letters, I see. From Vienna?'

Since nothing happened at the Schloss without the knowledge of Her Serene Highness, her son felt no obligation to make answer, but waited with weary resignation for her to continue, which she was not slow to do.

'I also have received a letter – from Countess von Deiter.'

'Well, I trust it is more entertaining than the one her

husband has written to me, which is, like the good Count himself, riddled with tedious verbosity.'

His sarcasm was not well received. The Dowager Princess had no great opinion of the new Secretary of State, but his wife was clever enough for the two of them – and had proved herself an admirable source of discreet confidences. Her Serene Highness' present grievance, however, centred upon her son's evasiveness. That one swift glance had established that there was no visible evidence of any letter bearing Baroness Raimund's fine distinctive scrawl, yet she knew for a fact that there had been such a letter, an unnecessarily thick one in her opinion.

'I found Irena von Deiter's letter profoundly disturbing,' she said coldly. 'Did you know that the house where Sophia is living is open to all the riff and raff? Really, Adolphus, I do feel that your man was most lax in his choice of accommodation. An appartment is quite unsuitable in my opinion, and Irena's letter does nothing to ease my fears. Fräulein Lanner has confided to her that your daughter is frequently jostled on the stairs by vulgar penniless musicians and is obliged to endure their odiously familiar greetings. As one might expect, Baroness Raimund refuses to take the matter seriously, which merely encourages the child to flout the Fräulein's authority.'

'Ah, I wondered when we should come to the nub of things,' said her son with equal coldness.

'Countess von Deiter is naturally concerned for Sophia, if only because any blemish in her character reflects in turn upon Gellenstadt. You should thank God that *she* at least cares!' There was no mistaking where this thrust was aimed.

'We are indebted to the Countess for her solicitude!' A brief burst of coughing shook the Prince's frail body. When it was spent he folded back the rug with fingers that shook and slowly stood up. His face, at its most austere, masked a great anger. How dare she attempt to interfere – to call his judgement into question?

'Mother, you oblige me to repeat what I had not thought to say again – namely that I placed all my confidence in Baroness Raimund when I entrusted Sophia to her care, and no amount of scurrilous tale-bearing will tempt me now to change my mind.'

*

In Vienna the gathering pace of events and the imminence of Sophia's Coming–Out ball left Lottie with little time to brood upon Prince Paul's shortcomings. In fact, a night's sleep had gone a long way to restoring her equilibrium and to persuading her that she had read far too much into what was no more than a moment of capriciousness on his part, best forgotten. For Sophia's sake, and because she had no wish to provoke more trouble, she resolved to behave towards him as though nothing had happened.

Her resolve had been put to the test on the following day when an extravagant floral offering was delivered, together with a card ambiguously expressing his thanks *for a delightful experience*.

'Roses!' Sophia exclaimed with innocent wonder. 'How lovely! And how extraordinary that Uncle Paul should have enjoyed the ballet so much. One would never have thought it at all his kind of thing!'

Lottie, with her face buried in the fragrant blooms to hide a sudden rush of colour, silently cursed his impudence as she murmured something indistinguishable.

Mr Annesley, who had been persuaded by his sister to accompany her and Mrs Osmond on their first visit to the Baroness, observed her reaction with some interest. Upon meeting her eyes he was further intrigued to find them filled with a kind of angry exasperation which quickly turned to confusion so that she immediately thrust the offending blooms into the arms of the footman who had brought them in, and shooed him out of the room with almost indecent haste.

'Well now.' Lottie took a deep breath and turned back to her visitors. 'This is very agreeable. Sophia, why don't you take Miss Annesley through to the music room where you may get to know one another at your leisure. Mrs Osmond, are you quite comfortable in that chair? If you would care to move nearer to the fire . . . ?'

'No, really, Baroness – I shall do very well here,' puffed the Annesleys' elderly relation, who had proved to be a small plump lady, a little too fussy for Lottie's taste, but good-hearted and clearly devoted to her young cousins. 'So kind . . .

and so very obliging of Her Royal Highness . . .' A few tentative chords followed by a sudden burst of laughter issued from the next room. 'There now!' she exclaimed. 'I declare I cannot recall when I last heard dear Alys so happy! Who knows, but it might not prove to be quite the best thing that has happened to her in a very long time! Do you not agree, Max?'

Maxim Annesley found himself wishing, not for the first time, that Cousin Carrie would express herself a little less effusively. Her lack of reservation made his own manner seem, by contrast, positively formal as he agreed with her, adding by way of a rider, 'However, we mustn't impose upon your good nature, ma'am, or that of Princess Sophia. I'm sure you must both have many engagements to fulfil.'

Lottie saw pride in the set of his jaw – a certain defensiveness, perhaps? Living with Mrs Osmond could not be easy for him, she thought, and sympathy with his predicament made her treat him with rather more generosity than she might otherwise have done.

'My dear sir, what nonsense!' she cried. 'I assure you, no one will be more pleased than I should your sister decide to honour us with her friendship. And as for Sophia – her upbringing has of necessity been a solitary affair, hedged about with tedious formality and protocol – not, you must agree, the ideal way for anyone to grow up. It is my earnest wish that the balance should be redressed a little while we are here. Perhaps,' she added tentatively, 'Alys might care to go about with us occasionally? And I do very much want you all to come to Sophia's ball since you have been so good as to give your blessing to our using the ballroom.'

There was an awkward pause, punctuated by a troubled 'Oh dear!' from Mrs Osmond. Mr Annesley cast her an impatient glance as he said, 'As to that – well, I'm not sure. I believe I mentioned to you my sister's dislike of company? She has, you see, a morbid fear of being looked upon as some kind of sideshow freak . . .'

Was the fear hers, Lottie wondered, or her brother's? Four years was a long time to be shut away in the country, shielded perhaps by an over-protective brother.

'But surely, sir, Miss Annesley cannot hold us in such poor esteem?'

'Oh, not you, dear Baroness!' exclaimed Mrs Osmond hastily. 'Never you! Why, from the moment Max told us of his having made your acquaintance Alys was all eagerness to meet you!'

'Really?' Lottie, much amused, turned to Mr Annesley in innocent enquiry, and found him for once less than urbane. The sunlight filled her eyes with dancing lights. 'My dear sir, what can you have said, I wonder, to have aroused so much lively curiosity in your sister's breast? No, don't tell me or you might put me to the blush. And here was I thinking that you had formed quite another opinion of me!'

His rueful grin acknowledged that the point was hers, and Mrs Osmond, looking from one to the other, was clearly pleased, if puzzled.

'But seriously, sir – ' Lottie continued.

'Seriously, ma'am, I cannot answer for my sister's feelings or wishes in this. The decision must be hers.' Mr Annesley stood up, his expression enigmatic but not unfriendly. 'And now, if you will permit, I shall leave the ladies in your care.' A sudden smile warmed his eyes. 'I have to see a man . . . about a pianoforte!'

She laughed. He really was quite human underneath that reserve, Lottie had decided as he departed, and since they were to live in close proximity, for the next few weeks, a harmonious relationship could only be to everyone's advantage.

In a matter of days Alys was somewhat surprised to find herself agreeing to take a drive in the Prater with her new-found friends. She was not quite sure how it had come about – one moment they were singing the praises of Vienna's most beautiful park and the next Sophia was saying with shy eagerness, 'Oh, do say you will come with us?' and Cousin Carrie was scurrying across the landing to return with her pelisse and bonnet, buttoning her up into the soft blue velvet with busy fingers and tying the ribbons of her bonnet into a fetching bow beneath one ear.

She looked enchanting, Lottie thought, but bewildered too – a little apprehensive, perhaps?

'My dear,' she said impulsively, 'You must not feel you have to come. We shan't be in the least offended, I promise you . . .'

Everything in Alys was urging her to take the avenue of

escape being offered to her; to cling to safety and security, to the loving care of Max and Cousin Carrie who knew exactly what to do for her, who could anticipate her every need. Her courage almost failed her.

Then she heard Lottie say in her warm encouraging way, 'The first step is always the hardest, I believe . . .' and she remembered why she had made the decision to come to Vienna – to make a bid for some measure of independence so that she might not be forever a burden upon Max.

There was hardly a tremor in her voice as she replied, 'How splendid of you to understand. And you are quite right. Of course I will come.'

Mrs Osmond declined to accompany them, pleading that she had letters to write. 'I seem to be for ever behindhand with my correspondence, and I know that Alys will be in good hands!' As she prepared to take her leave, she confided to Lottie, 'You cannot know how pleased this makes me! And you must not mind the way Max guards her. It is only natural in the circumstances that he should wish to protect the child . . . though he is motivated solely by love and not guilt as some cruel tongues would have it!' This was said with a fierceness that made Lottie quite unbearably curious.

But already the old lady was chattering on. 'Still, that is neither here nor there now. I have always maintained that if Alys had not overheard some rather cruel remark soon after the accident . . . the fall left her rather bruised for a time and gels of sixteen are highly sensitive, are they not? . . . but if it had not been so, she would not have chosen to live so close retired . . . Ah, there you are, my love!' Her voice changed dramatically as the Princess and Alys came back into the room. 'There now! Did you ever see a more charming sight, Baroness? How very fine they look together!'

It was true. Sophia had chosen a pelisse in a rich brown that made her dark eyes sparkle, and with her shining curls peeping from beneath the poke of her bonnet, she was a perfect foil for Alys' almost ethereal fairness, and although the smaller and younger of the two, she looked every inch a princess.

Presently the Gellenstadt carriage with its royal crest proudly emblazoned on the shabby coachwork was rattling and swaying along busy streets teeming with a colourful throng.

'Oh, I do wish you could see it all!' Sophie exclaimed with a complete absence of embarrassment.

Lottie sent her a reproving glance, but Alys only smiled.

'You shall describe it to me,' she said. 'Max is quite good at doing so, but gentlemen, you know, don't notice all the little things.'

Sophia needed no second bidding. 'Well, for a start there are soldiers everywhere, quite splendid in every imaginable kind of uniform! But even they are not so splendid as the ladies in their beautiful dresses . . . you never saw such silks and satins, and ostrich plumes and the *prettiest* parasols . . . and there are simply swarms of servants to attend them, in the finest livery . . . rich blues and purples and black, with miles of silver and gold lace! There are magnificent carriages, too, and all the grandest ones have lackeys to run before them, swinging great silver-knobbed canes. They look so funny . . . as if they are flying!'

At last Sophia was obliged to pause for breath, and Lottie, who had been listening and watching rather anxiously, was relieved to hear a soft chuckle from Alys.

'Yes, you are a decided improvement upon Max!'

They were by now approaching the island on the Danube where a wide avenue of immense chestnut trees stretched invitingly, as though bidding the Viennese and their illustrious visitors to explore its dappled shade. Soon, the main avenue became criss-crossed by others, all alive with carriages of every kind, while on the great swards of green lawns a colourful array of people strolled in the autumn sunshine amid a soft hum of conversation.

'It has always seemed to me,' said Lottie, 'that everything here has been orchestrated into a most delightful symphony of sound and movement.'

Sophia giggled – an engagingly youthful sound. 'On my first visit, I couldn't believe my eyes! There were so many people. I had expected it to be like our own little park at home, but the Prater is of so great an expanse!'

Alexei Metlin, having discharged his not very arduous duties to the Czar, was also taking the air in the company of friends. It had already become clear to him that the Congress would occasion him much pleasure. So many pretty women, so many agreeable balls, so many opportunities for flirtations of the most delightful kind. The sight of the Gellenstadt equipage ahead of him on the adjacent avenue seemed to give point to his reflections. The touch of a spur set his mount caracolling playfully before setting off at a brisk trot.

It was Sophia, with her back to the horses, who saw him coming. Her soft 'Oh!' and blush of confusion made Lottie glance back. With a sigh of resignation she ordered Humbert to stop.

'Ladies!' The prince drew abreast of them and reined in. 'This is a pleasure indeed!' His tawny eyes glinted with merriment and Lottie was struck yet again by the curious attraction in the crooked smile and luxuriant red-gold whiskers, so that she found her own mouth curving irrepressibly in response. His glance moved to where Alys sat unmoving, looking straight ahead, and then returned to Lottie, his eyebrow expressively quirked.

She nodded and a quick rush of sympathy warmed his eyes. 'Will you not introduce me to your most charming companion, Baroness?' he said with just the right degree of interest, and proceeded to put her at ease with an experience that drew Lottie's admiration, for he did so without for one instant neglecting Sophia or herself.

They were all in high good humour when Prince Paul presently rode up. His arrival coincided with some particular witticism so that his first sight was of Lottie laughing up at Alexei Metlin from beneath the sweeping brim of her stylish hat, exquisite poise in the tilt of her head. The violence of his reaction surprised even himself, and his eyes held a dangerous glitter as he greeted her.

Lottie could not but notice that look and the oddest little shiver ran along her nerves. It gave an added challenge to the look she returned him.

She made Alys known to him, and he responded with a curtness that seemed to make her shrink back a little into her corner. Lottie was furious.

'Prince Alexei was enlarging upon his plans for a picnic in the woods above Vienna,' she said, her own objections to the venture taking instant flight as she struggled to contain her anger. 'We thought perhaps Wednesday,' she added pugnaciously.

Since but a moment ago she had been demurring as to the wisdom of the venture, this earned her a quizzical look from Metlin and a joyous exclamation of surprise from Sophia. She leaned forward, her shyness forgotten, and clapped her hands. 'You have changed your mind! Oh, I am so pleased. It sounds such fun! Will you come too, Uncle Paul? Do say that you will!'

With narrowed eyes Paul watched the myriad emotions chase across Lottie's face. A gleam of amusement flickered briefly. 'I wonder if I should,' he mused. 'Perhaps Baroness Lottie would prefer that I decline?'

Sophia stared. 'No. I'm sure you are wrong. He may come, mayn't he, Baroness?'

Lottie swallowed back the retort that leaped to her lips and said airily, 'My dear child, your uncle is at perfect liberty to do as he pleases! I have no power to order him!'

Alexei looked from one to the other. He was not a fool. There was a degree of friction between them that must arouse curiosity. He said amiably, 'Then it is for Wednesday. I shall arrange everything.'

The three young ladies returned home from this excursion with mixed feelings; Lottie, still simmering a little over Prince Paul's behaviour, had attempted to apologize to Alys for his apparent lack of manners, but had been assured that no such apology was necessary. In an odd sort of way, his very offhandedness had had a bracing effect upon her which in retrospect was not entirely unpleasing. Sophia was quite unaware of any lapse on her uncle's part, being lost in contemplation of the picnic to come.

Alys was certainly looking much less tense as she was helped down from the carriage. With Lottie's hand unobtrusively guiding her, she made her way with growing confidence towards the entrance. They had just reached the stairway when all kinds of things seemed to happen at once.

Tasha uttered an excited yelp which was immediately answered by a deep-throated bark and a rush of feet as a huge dark shape erupted from the basement steps and hurled itself upon them. Alys froze, all her old fears returning as from the direction of the stairs came yet more footsteps coming down fast – at least two people, she judged.

Lottie hardly knew which way to turn first – reluctant to let go of Alys, whose panic she could feel rising, yet assailed by the urgent need to secure Tasha who had slipped her leash and was even now making the most blatant overtures to her admirer, an enormous shaggy creatures with pricked ears and bright questing eyes who clearly accepted her homage as his due. Just like a man!

'Tasha . . . come here at once!' she exclaimed. 'Alys, I'm sorry, but I must leave you for just a moment. If you stand quite still, you'll come to no harm. Sophia, do see if you can rescue Tasha's lead!' And, as the spaniel continued to behave in the most grovelling way, 'Oh, you ridiculous dog! Why can't you be more discriminating?'

As Alys stood, not daring to move amid the ensuing pandemonium, two new voices intervened, both masculine but one deeper than the other and full of laughter. He it was who took charge of the proceedings and though she could not understand what he or his friend said, within moments order had been restored.

'It is our pleasure, *Gnädige* Baroness.'

Alys heard the faint click of heels as the young men introduced themselves to Lottie as Ferdie Graber and Lorenz Bergen, and explained that they were musicians who shared one of the attic rooms. And then he was standing in front of Alys, taking her trembling hand in his and saying in the most endearing fractured English, 'Do not be afraid, gracious and beautiful lady. It is but two foolish young dogs. It would seem that they too have their passions! See – the wicked fellow is come to make his *Salut*!'

Perhaps it was the gentleness of his voice, combined with the hound's friendly whine and the familiar feel of a large shaggy body rubbing against her in a way that reminded her of her own dear dogs at home, but quite suddenly with one hand still imprisoned in Herr Graber's and the fingers of the other buried in the hound's rough coat, all her fears melted away.

And Lottie, seeing them together, the too thin young man with a shock of curling hair and wearing spectacles, and Alys with her delicate quiescent beauty, was instantly aware that she was witnessing something special, and a little shiver of excitement ran up into her hair.

*

Alys was at her dressing table when Max knocked and came in. He crossed the room and stood behind her, and as so often, the sweet perfection of her reflection seemed to mock him.

'Are you all right, love?'

Her smile was a little abstracted. 'Yes, of course. What makes you ask?'

'Carrie said you had been driving in the Prater with the Baroness. I just wondered . . .

She lifted her face towards him. 'Everything was fine. I suddenly decided that I had been a coward for long enough.'

'You mustn't ever say such things about yourself!' Max put his hands on her shoulders and drew her back against him. 'I visited Dr Strauss this afternoon. He is willing to see you on Wednesday.'

The day of the picnic, she thought inconsequentially. How fortunate that I declined Prince Alexei's invitation.

There was no change in her expression, but he felt a slight tremor run through her and at once his hold tightened comfortingly.

'Dearest girl, you don't have to go if you don't want to! No one knows about it – not even Carrie.'

'No, and I don't want anyone to know,' she said quickly. 'They will ask questions and I shall feel such a fool if . . .' This time it was she who felt his distress. She put up a hand to touch his face and said reassuringly, 'Oh, I'm not expecting miracles – truly, but we both agreed, from the moment you first heard about Dr Strauss, that I should consult him at the earliest opportunity, and nothing has happened to make me change my mind. If he can help me, I shall be overjoyed, but if not, I am no worse off than before.'

Except, she added to herself, that I do so want to see what Ferdie Graber looks like. Wishful thinking was an indulgence she had never until now permitted herself, but this time no amount of schooling could still her traitorous thoughts.

4

Even before Sophia's ball, Lottie's drawing rooms were on the way to being counted among Vienna's most fashionable venues. Princess Metternich might receive on Mondays, Princess Trautmansdorf on Thursdays and Countess Zichy on Saturdays, but the word soon spread that one might visit Baroness Raimund at any time and be sure of a warm welcome and congenial company free from the more opulent formality to be found among these doyennes of Viennese society, and mercifully devoid of political discussion.

'Really, my dear,' said Lady Merrivale when Lottie finally made good her promise to visit, 'you have made a *succès fou*! I scarcely go anywhere but your name is on someone's lips.'

Lottie laughed. 'Ah, but what are they saying, ma'am? That is more to the point.'

'Nothing but good, I assure you!' Lady Merrivale's statuesque figure puffed with a kind of shared pride. 'Is that not so, Arabella?'

'If you say so, Mama,' sighed Lady Merrivale's elder daughter. 'For my part, I never listen to idle gossip.' She paused in her restless wanderings about the room to study her reflection in a mirror near the window with every appearance of complacence, well pleased with the peach-bloom ruching that lined the high poke of her bonnet and cast such a becoming glow; from there she passed on to glance out of the window with a trace of impatience. 'Lady Sarah is late,' she said.

Lottie admitted that there was much to admire in Miss Merrivale; the flawless features and creamy skin, the glossy black hair that shone like spun silk, and a superb figure that Sophia, only two years her junior, sighed over with some envy. It was a pity that one couldn't like her more. She wondered briefly how serious Max Annesley's intentions were towards Arabella – surely he couldn't be unaware of her rather pitying attitude towards his sister.

As if prompted by these thoughts, Arabella said grudgingly,

'Max says you have already wrought wonders with poor Alys.'

'I have done nothing for Alys beyond making her feel welcome,' Lottie returned crisply. 'Any small victories Alys has achieved are solely of her own making!'

'Well, whoever is responsible, Max must be relieved to see her going about more. She cannot expect to hang for ever like a millstone about his neck.'

Lottie was furious, and even Lady Merrivale looked uncomfortable and reproached her daughter gently.

'Well, I'm sorry, Mama,' said Arabella, sounding not the least repentant. 'But it does affect Max's eligibility as a husband, notwithstanding that his prospects are so fine, for no wife will wish to have a blind girl for ever about the place!' She looked out of the window once more and her whole demeanour changed. 'The carriage has arrived. I must go! Forgive me, Baroness, but I am going for a drive with Lady Sarah Bingley and must not keep her waiting!'

There was a pregnant silence in the room when she had gone. Finally Lady Merrivale said in a rather strained voice, 'My dear Charlotte, I beg you will not refine too much upon what Arabella said. It is but a phase. To tell the truth, she is become rather too close with this Lady Sarah Bingley, who is considerably older than Bella and not quite all that one would wish! There was some hint of scandal a month or two back . . . but one must not heed all one hears. I daresay most of it is wildly exaggerated!' Her ladyship sighed. 'However, I fear she is not having a very good influence upon Bella, but you know how it is: the child is flattered by the attentions of a sophisticated woman and will hear nothing against her. One can only hope that the acquaintance will quickly run its course, and that Lady Bingley's influence will pall before too much damage is done.'

Lottie felt obliged to agree with what reassurance she could muster, though she privately felt less than sympathetic. To change the subject she asked, 'Is Max Annesley really so eligible a *parti*?'

'Goodness, yes! Did you not know? His uncle is the Earl of Stanton – one of the richest men in England, and Max is his heir! Such a pity that he has taken his sister's tragic disability so much to heart.'

'Forgive me, ma'am, but something I have heard has made me wonder . . .' Lottie hated herself for yielding to the temptation to quiz the older woman, yet an irresistible force drove her on. 'It was the merest hint . . . that there might be some feeling of guilt on his part?'

'Wicked speculation!' exclaimed her ladyship forcefully. 'It is true that he has always blamed himself for what happened, but I fail to see how he could have prevented the accident, when the child – for Alys was but sixteen at the time – took out his new, scarce-broken hunter against his express wishes! However, that is the kind of man Max is . . . he had been both loving brother and guardian to Alys for many years, and to suggest that his devotion to her since the accident is anything less laudable than that is what I can't be doing with!'

Lady Merrivale's vehemence was touching and gave Lottie a great deal more insight into the relationship that clearly existed between brother and sister, so that she resolved more than ever to do all she could to help.

The day of the picnic dawned fine and clear, and Sophia was quite pale with excitement – so much so that Fräulein Lanner, who had never approved the outing despite the inclusion of Prince Paul, whom she considered to be but a pale shadow of his brother, was all for preventing Sophia from participating.

'It is pure folly, Baroness,' the cold voice intoned. 'With Her Royal Highness' début but a day or two away, to be risking exposure to chills, or worse! It is not the time for picnics.'

'Nonsense,' Lottie insisted, her voice pleasant but firm. 'An afternoon in the fresh air will benefit the Princess far more than sitting stuffily indoors. We should make use of the sunshine while we may, for winter will be with us soon enough.'

Alys had steadfastly refused to accompany them, and in the end had become so distressed by Sophia's attempts to persuade her that Lottie was obliged to step in and put an end to her misery.

Prince Alexei arrived promptly, presenting himself, with Prince Paul, for the privilege of escorting the ladies down to the carriage – or rather, carriages, for there were three standing in line to await their coming. Lottie laughed aloud at so much extravagance, but he only protested good-naturedly that it was impossible to manage with less.

Prince Paul said little, but she was very much aware that his eyes were raking her from head to toe; only the knowledge that he could have little fault to find with her appearance enabled her to withstand his scrutiny. She had chosen the close-fitting ivory redingote primarily for the warmth of its thick velvet pile and high-fastening sable collar, but she was not unaware that it was also exceedingly becoming and of the first style, with its matching sable-trimmed toque set jauntily upon her coiffured head.

Sophia, in her favourite shade of amber with swansdown at the neck and edging the brim of a close-fitting bonnet, was incoherent and enchanting as she was helped into the first of the three carriages, but by the time they had passed through several tiny hamlets and were climbing steadily to the heights of the Kahlenburg she had recovered her tongue sufficiently to respond shyly to Prince Alexei whose ease of manner soon had her conversing with growing confidence, and exclaiming over the scenery, so that by the time they reached their destination she had quite forgotten to be shy.

'Oh!' she exclaimed softly as she stepped down and turned to look about her. And indeed, whichever way one looked, the view was breathtaking – Lottie had forgotten just how breathtaking. There were huge beech trees glowing red-gold in the autumn sunshine, and looking between their serried ranks one could see deeper and lighter patches of rich purple and scarlet and yellow, where oak and maple and elm grew, while here and there, trapped in the light, came the silvery shiver of aspens. Almost directly opposite was the Leopolsberg, which formed the twin spur of the Wienerwald. Here black pines rose up dramatically from limestone cliffs and far below, cradled between them with a grace that must surely be unmatched anywhere else, lay the city spreading outwards from the walled centre in a pattern of roads and parks and gardens, with here and there a glint of water.

'It is like home,' Sophia breathed. 'But so much bigger!'

There was laughter at this, most of it kindly, for Sophia's lack of sophistication touched a chord in all but the most cynical of hearts.

The party included several people unknown to Lottie – dashing young officers from Alexei's regiment and two exquisite creatures whose function was clearly to look beautiful and please the gentlemen since they hardly touched the delicious food and at no time showed the least interest in the conversation. She was also afforded her first glimpse of Lady Sarah Bingley, and saw at once why Lady Merrivale was so troubled; a curvaceous beauty of some thirty summers whose dress bespoke Paris in every line, Lady Sarah nevertheless had hard eyes and was well suited in her companion, von Gratz.

Lottie had been none too pleased to find the Duke one of the party, but he seemed absorbed by the lady, and her fears soon subsided. Prince Paul was equally preoccupied with his most recent conquest, a well-endowed young brunette, so she was soon able to forget them and enjoy herself.

The spot chosen by Alexei was well sheltered, there were servants to lay out all manner of delicacies, and the champagne, dispensed with a liberality that quite took Lottie's breath away, bubbled and sparkled to create a merry mood.

'The little one is clearly enjoying herself.'

Prince Alexei's voice was comically doleful as he watched Sophia surrounded by young men and put at her ease by the light-hearted extravagance of their compliments. 'I am quite eclipsed!'

'Poor you!' Lottie leaned back on her hands and laughed down at him where he sprawled beside her. 'I would feel sorry for you were I not certain that you are well content. And to be honest, at the moment I would rather see Sophia with half a dozen suitors than just one.'

His eyes crinkled into a quizzical grin. 'I thought you might, but it is a severe blow to my pride, you understand. I shall need much comforting if I am to rally!'

'I'm sure you will have little difficulty, dear sir, in finding someone not only willing but positively eager to assuage your grief!'

'You are a hard woman, Baroness!' he sighed and closed his eyes upon the echo of her laughter.

Lottie was content to sit quietly for a while, her eyes closed against the dappled sunlight, letting the sound flow around her, not wanting the day to end. When she opened them again,

Alexei was fast asleep beside her – and Sophia was no longer with the group of young men. She sat forward abruptly, and with a twist of dismay saw that von Gratz had appropriated her and removed her a little way from the rest. He towered above her, making her look tinier than ever, and fragile – a dove to his eagle. He was doing most of the talking, dominating her with his particular brand of arrogant predatory charm, and even at a distance Lottie could discern two spots of colour bright against the pallor of Sophia's cheeks as she listened with lowered eyes.

Lottie's first instinct was to rush across and rescue her, but a moment's reflection persuaded her that less attention would be drawn to the child if her uncle were to intervene.

She looked about her and saw that he too had moved away from the rest, and stood alone, leaning with negligent grace against a giant beech trunk, wrapped in a long caped driving coat, arms folded. He lifted lazy eyelids in mock surprise as she approached, and the glitter in his eyes suggested that he might have imbibed a little too freely of the champagne.

'What's this, lovely Lottie? Am I to be forgiven?'

She ignored the sarcasm and came straight to the point. 'Did you arrange for von Gratz to be here today?' she demanded.

His brow quirked. 'My dear girl, this is Metlin's affair, not mine.'

'Don't prevaricate, Highness. You have only to use your eyes to see what is happening! Even you must be aware that Sophia is no match for a man like that! As her uncle, the very least you can do is to go over there and lend her your protection.'

'Ah!' He wagged a finger at her. 'But I'm not her guardian, *Gnädige* Baroness. My illustrious brother granted that privilege to you!'

Lottie was growing desperate. She glanced over her shoulder just in time to see the Duke put a hand masterfully under Sophia's chin. 'But von Gratz is your friend,' she pleaded. 'And you do care for Sophia just a little, surely? You wouldn't wish to see her importuned?'

'Importuned?' He invested the word with heavy irony.

'Well, what else would you call it?' Lottie could have

screamed with frustration. 'Oh, for heaven's sake, stop playing games! I am well aware that it would suit you very well for Sophia to marry your friend, but Prince Adolphus would never permit it, and well you know it!'

'Still guarding my dear brother's interests?' he sneered.

'If you like,' she snapped back. 'The fact is that while we are in Vienna, I stand in place of Sophia's father!'

'That must give you a great feeling of power,' he drawled, and straightened up suddenly – so suddenly that involuntarily she stepped back a pace, and then felt foolish. 'Come for a walk,' he said, making it sound more like an order than an invitation.

'I think you're drunk!' she said accusingly.

'Wrong,' he said, his eyes glinting. 'Were I drunk, you would be in no doubt about it.'

'Well, if you won't rescue your niece from that brute, I will!'

Paul's jaw tightened. Without a word he strode across the clearing, his coat swirling about him as he ruthlessly ploughed through the remains of the picnic, scattering the servants who were busy tidying up and packing things away.

Lottie followed, at a more decorous pace, exchanging a despairing glance with Alexei, who was by now fully awake and had just become aware of what was going on.

'If he makes a scene and draws attention to Sophia, I'll kill him!' she muttered wrathfully. 'The whole thing is probably his fault in the first place! He just can't resist the temptation to meddle!'

She was too preoccupied to notice the surprised look Prince Alexei gave her, or to heed his apologetic: 'I should have been more watchful. The little one is no match for our bold Duke!' For Prince Paul had reached von Gratz, was flinging an arm affectionately around Sophia and saying with an insouciance she had not thought possible in his present mood, 'So this is where you've been hiding, *Liebling*. Dammit, but you're a sly fellow, Franz. I'll have you know this child promised to take her old uncle for a walk. I hope you mean to yield her gracefully!'

Just for a moment Lottie was aware of tension in the air. The Duke's face darkened, the brutal chin lifted dangerously, and then he laughed, tapped Sophia's face with one finger, and bowed formally over her hand. 'So be it,' he said. 'There will be other times, yes? '

She didn't answer, couldn't answer; prayed desperately that he had not noticed how she flinched ever so slightly when he touched her – and watched his retreating back with a relief that threatened to swamp her.

'Sophia!'

It was her uncle's voice, bracing – almost savage in her ear. The sound steadied her, forced her to pull herself together, except that when she tried to speak her teeth began to chatter uncontrollably.

'Devil take it, Metlin, the child is chilled to the bone,' Prince Paul said harshly. 'Find her a rug or a wrap or something, for pity's sake!'

'At once.'

'Perhaps you should go and rest in the carriage for a while, my dear,' said Lottie matter-of-factly. 'Fräulein Lanner will delight to say "I told you so", if you take a chill.'

'No!' said Sophia with a touch of panic. 'I d-don't want to rest . . . to be alone!'

'Of course you don't,' agreed her uncle. 'You want to take a walk with me. Baroness Lottie has already refused me her company, and if you mean to be equally cruel – ' his eyes, bright and hard as flint, flicked to meet Lottie's and back ' – I shall probably go into a decline!'

Sophia instinctively straightened her shoulders and gave a hiccuping little laugh. He nodded approvingly, relieved to note that she had lost that dreadful blank look which had reminded him uncomfortably of a rabbit he had once seen, frozen into immobility by a snake.

Compassion was an emotion quite new to Paul, and he wasn't at all sure that he liked the sensations it evoked; even less did he like being made an object of Lottie Raimund's censure, as if he had deliberately encouraged Franz to . . . what was that ridiculous word she had used? . . . *importune* his niece! There was no doubt in his mind that Franz von Gratz would make an ideal husband for Sophia – strong, ambitious, in a privileged position close to the throne of Bavaria. What Franz lacked, unfortunately, was the least hint of subtlety in his bid to secure Sophia's consent and trust. He would need to have words with him.

'Come now, *dushka*.' Alexei was back, carrying a sable wrap which he made show of arranging. 'This will have you warm in no time!'

'Splendid,' said Prince Paul. 'Let's go then.'

Sophia, snuggling into the wrap, threw them all a tremulous smile, already almost recovered, and Lottie felt a curious sense of rejection as she saw the eagerness with which the Princess turned to her uncle, and as they strode away together, he with his arm flung carelessly about her shoulders, the feeling resolved itself into an angry constriction in her throat.

5

Sophia's ball was a triumph. Almost everyone agreed that there had never been anything quite like it – and that it was quite the most brilliant affair of the Congress to date, for although there had perhaps been grander balls, none had achieved so beguiling an atmosphere.

Even Countess von Deiter could not fault the arrangements – though Lottie was sure she must have tried hard and long to find *some* cause for complaint! Lottie had been aware from the first that not only would her own reputation as a hostess be under scrutiny, but that the ball would be seen as a reflection of Grand Prince Adolphus zu Bayersdorf-Gellenstadt's standard of hospitality, so she was at great pains to ensure that everything was as it should be.

In this she was greatly supported by Josef. It was several years since he had been called upon to prepare for so important a function – indeed, he doubted whether his late master, the Baron, had ever attempted anything quite so prestigious, but he was determined that the Baroness should not find him wanting. Extra servants were engaged, and set to scrub and sweep the vast gilded ballroom; to wash and polish the mirrors that ran the length of the room until they gleamed, reflecting the lustres of the chandeliers that on the night would be lit by hundreds of tapers. An orchestra was hired and a military band to play during supper; extra chefs, the best that Vienna could provide, spent hours and days in the steaming kitchens preparing delicacies fit to grace the palates of great diplomatic and court personages – and perhaps even a royalty or two.

For once Lottie was grateful to Fraülein Lanner, whose rigid adherence to discipline kept Sophia from becoming too excited. The child seemed none the worse for her experience and it was to be hoped that Duke Franz would have taken the hint.

'I cannot forbid him the ball,' she had explained matter-of-factly to the Princess. 'He is your uncle's friend, and has been invited, though I suppose we may always hope that he will think better of coming!'

'I shan't mind if he does come,' Sophia had returned with a lofty self-possession that made Lottie reflect wryly upon the resilience of the young. 'Uncle Paul promised me that I shall not have to dance with the Duke if I don't want to.' She looked gravely at Lottie. 'Isn't it odd? I never thought that I should like Uncle Paul half so well as I do. He used to say such withering things to me when I was small! I think, perhaps,' she smiled, 'he doesn't like small children much.'

It was on the tip of Lottie's tongue to suggest that a niece of marriagable age was a negotiable commodity, but decided that it would be needlessly unkind to deprive the child of her illusions.

There had been some element of doubt as to whether the Annesleys would, after all, attend the ball. The day following the picnic Mrs Osmond had called to tell them that Alys would not be paying her usual visit.

'I hope she is not unwell?' Lottie said.

'My dear, I'm sure I don't know what to make of her. Hardly a word has she uttered either last evening or this morning.' Mrs Osmond sighed. 'Max says she'll come about and I'm not to fuss . . . as if I would!'

Lottie, obliged to hide a smile, said that Mr Annesley was probably right. 'We all have moments when we don't feel sociable, after all.'

'I'm sure I cannot imagine you ever feeling that way, dear Baroness,' gushed Mrs Osmond. 'But there's no denying that Alys is not herself. Properly in the suds! And just when everything was going so well, too!'

Lottie was not unsympathetic, but her mind began to wander to the thousand and one jobs waiting to be done. The good lady appeared to be comfortably settled in her chair for some time to come and Lottie was at a loss as to how to get rid of her without giving offence. She was saved when, in the middle of a long peroration which seemed to be largely concerned with the delicacy of her young cousin's constitution following upon her accident, Josef came in to say that Prince Metlin had called.

'There . . . I must not keep you from your friends,' Mrs Osmond puffed, extricating her plump figure with some difficulty from the many cushions with which she had surrounded herself, and throwing Prince Alexei an arch look as he entered and hurried forward to her assistance.

'Do give Alys my dearest love,' Lottie said warmly. 'We shall not intrude, of course, but if she would like Sophia or myself to call, you have but to let me know.'

'Thank you, my friend,' she said as the door closed behind her verbose visitor, and she was able to turn at last to Alexei, her eyes brimming with mirth. 'She is a dear soul, but a little of her goes a very long way!'

'I hope Miss Annesley is not unwell?' he asked.

'Not precisely unwell, I think. Just a little mopish.'

He smiled his crooked smile. 'Suffering from a surfeit of words, perhaps?' He accepted a glass of Madeira from Josef, who had returned unobtrusively bearing a tray. 'I came to enquire after the Princess. She is none the worse for our little expedition, I trust? When I saw that she was not with you I felt some alarm.'

'No, Sophia is fine,' Lottie reassured him. 'She is with her governess at present – they do an hour or so of work most mornings.'

Alexei wrinkled his nose, and she laughed.

'Yes, I know. But it does her no harm, and makes Fräulein Lanner feel wanted! As to what happened . . .' She shrugged. 'I think it is best forgotten. I don't know what Prince Paul said to her, but whatever it was seems to have had a beneficial effect.'

When Lottie later met Max Annesley on the stair, she was quick to enquire after Alys. His manner was distant and she felt a pang of disappointment, for it had seemed that they were on the way to becoming much better acquainted. But when he spoke, she realized that much of his restraint stemmed from concern for his sister.

'Her distress is of a very private nature, ma'am – and as such, she cannot bring herself to discuss it with anyone at present. Even our cousin is not privy to her thoughts. But this mood *will* pass.' He seemed almost to be convincing himself, and Lottie's heart at once went out to him. 'If you can but be patient, Alys will soon be herself again. In time she may even feel able to confide in you.' There was a fleeting anguish in his eyes as he concluded tautly, 'She sorely needs someone other than myself . . . a woman closer to her in age than Carrie. There are times, I fear, when I am not enough – '

'I am sure that is not true!' Lottie exclaimed passionately. 'I know how deeply Alys cares for you, and relies upon you!'

'Yes, of course.' He was clearly embarrassed by his outburst, and his manner became formal once more. 'Tell Her Royal Highness as much as you think fit. I think she would do well not to count upon Alys being able to attend her ball.'

But in the event, Alys recovered rather more quickly than her brother had anticipated, and though she was much more subdued than usual, she avowed her intention to attend the ball.

'If I may just sit quietly at the back somewhere?' she said. 'So that I may listen to the music without . . . without troubling anyone.'

Sophia opened her mouth to protest, but Lottie lifted a warning hand, and she shut it again.

'You may do exactly as you please, my dear,' she said lightly, and watched the tiny frown ease from Alys' brow.

'Thank you. Oh, by the way, did you know that Herr Graber is to play in the orchestra you have engaged for your ball?'

The casual manner of the question was belied by the faint tide of colour that ran up under the pallor of the young girl's skin. Lottie, much intrigued, was equally casual as she replied that she did not.

'You will be wondering how I know, I daresay?' Alys said diffidently.

'I expect you have had a secret assignation with Herr Graber,' Sophia declared dramatically, and as the tide of colour deepened a little, she clapped her hands. 'Why, I believe that is it!'

'Don't be a tease, Sophia!' Lottie admonished, lest Alys took fright and said no more. 'Take no notice of her, my dear,' she reassured Alys. 'Those young men are for ever up and down the stairs, so it doesn't at all surprise me if you have bumped into them again.'

'It was something like that,' Alys admitted. 'I met Herr Graber when I was going out with Max last Wednesday. My brother had to come back upstairs for some papers, and he was kind enough to stay and talk to me. It is quite extraordinary how hard both he and his friend work, you know. They are in the state orchestra, but must take all kinds of other work besides in order to make sufficient money, so they play for balls and concerts, and give pianoforte lessons in their spare time . . . and as if that were not enough, Herr Graber also composes music. That is what he wishes to do, more than anything else: to become a great composer!'

It was an unexpectedly animated little speech, and Lottie wondered if Alys knew how much it betrayed her. For those few moments her delicate face was vibrant with life, her figure, even in its customary attitude of stillness, seeming eager and oddly vulnerable. Well, well, she thought. What would Max have to say to such a friendship? One thing was apparent – whatever ailed Alys, it was in no way connected with her interest in Ferdie Graber.

On the evening of the ball it very soon became clear that the whole household was resolved to enter into the spirit of the proceedings with a gaiety that only the Viennese could achieve. The basement dwellers wore their finery and formed a motley guard of honour, greeting each new arrival with enthusiastic cheers and entertaining themselves betweentimes. The family on the third floor sat on the stairs above, well supplied with wine and cheeses, and their children peered wide-eyed through the banister rails at the glittering scene below. And an artist who shared the attics with Ferdie and Lorenz found himself an unobtrusive corner near the head of the staircase where he was soon busy executing lightning sketches of the notables as they arrived, in the hope that he might be able to sell some of them later.

Josef could do nothing about it. He poured out his despair to Lottie, but she only laughed and said, 'Why shouldn't everyone enjoy themselves?' And that if nothing worse than that happened, she would be vastly relieved.

In Sophia's bedchamber what seemed like an army of seamstresses and lady's maids, hairdressers and assorted helpers milled about jabbering ceaselessly and defying all attempts by the indomitable Fräulein Lanner to control them. In their midst stood the Princess, looking pale and saying that she felt sick and must surely swoon.

'Nonsense!' said Lottie. 'Take some deep breaths and then look in the mirror and tell me how such a vision can possibly contemplate anything so sordid as feeling sick!'

Sophia obeyed mutely and, brought face to face with her reflection, could scarcely believe her eyes, for she seemed to be floating in a diaphanous cloud of white spider gauze shot through with silver threads which caught the light whenever she moved. The brief bodice and tiny puff sleeves emphasized the slightness of her figure, and the hairdresser had most skilfully affixed her Crown Princess' diadem amid the dark gleaming curls piled high *à la Greque*. The result was magical, and unconsciously her head lifted in a gesture that was truly regal, all thoughts of swooning forgotten.

'Well, Fräulein?' Lottie demanded triumphantly, aware that for once the governess could have no possible fault to find. 'Have I done well?'

Fräulein Lanner nodded grudgingly, unable to bring herself to frame a reply.

'Now, Sophia . . . stay exactly as you are while I complete my toilette!' Lottie implored, and then, fearing that the Fräulein might unsettle her – 'No, come with me. I will not keep you above two minutes.'

Still in her wrapper, Lottie hurried back to her own room, where she was chivvied and scolded by her maid Gertrude, who was privately of the opinion that her own mistress would far outshine the Princess, if only she would not skimp on essentials. 'Rush, rush, rush!' she muttered as Lottie deftly completed her skilful application of rouge and flicked the hare'sfoot over her face before shedding the wrap and allowing herself to be helped into her own gown. 'You want that you should be seen at your best also, don't you?'

Gertrude tweaked and pulled and fastened and finally stood back critically. '*Ja*!' She gave a little nod of satisfaction and an enigmatic, 'It is as I thought!'

'Oh, Baroness Lottie . . . you are very fine!' Sophia exclaimed.

The slim classic robe of rose pink silk worn over a slip of silver tissue was cut low at the neck and edged with silver lace, the sleeves slashed and inset with the same. The colour did wonderful things to her hair which the hairdresser had brushed and pomaded into glossy side curls at the front while the rest was swept up and caught into a handsome opera comb set with sapphires and diamonds. Otto's sapphires echoed the blue of her eyes, making them sparkle, and her satin slippers and gloves exactly matched her gown.

She turned away, well satisfied, and took a small package from her dressing table.

'This is from your father, my dear. He had it specially designed for you.'

Sophia tore away the wrapping with trembling fingers and opened the little casket to reveal a silver filigree necklet, cobweb-fine, the incredible delicacy of its design incorporating the Gellenstadt crest.

'I am sure I have never seen anything so beautiful!' she breathed as Gertrude secured the catch for her.

'And this is but a mere trifle from me, my love.' Lottie's gift was a small ornamental fan of silver lace and ivory.

In the drawing room more delights awaited Sophia; her uncle had arrived early and was standing with one foot on the fender, a glass cradled negligently in one hand, as he stared pensively into the fire. He swung round as they came in, and Lottie thought inconsequentially that there was nothing to quite equal the sight of an officer of hussars in full dress uniform, extravagantly embroidered and braided, and when it was worn, as now by Prince Paul, with a devil-may-care elegance, and with the added distinction of the pale blue and gold sash of Gellenstadt, the effect was enough to render any but the most level-headed of women (of which she thanked God she was one) almost insensible with delight!

He bowed to them both with exquisite formality. 'Behold, I am here to do my duty for niece and country.' Then he kissed Sophia on both cheeks and informed her that she was looking utterly adorable and that were he not her uncle, he would fall in love with her on the instant.

She laughed, delighting in the compliment. 'But Baroness Lottie looks quite as beautiful, don't you think?'

And Lottie was obliged to stand while his unsparing eyes took in every minute detail of her appearance, from head to toe. She waited, chin high, for the usual mocking comment, but although there was an enigmatic smile in his eyes, he said only: 'Oh, quite as beautiful!' which could not possibly account for the sudden quickening of her pulse.

'And see, Uncle Paul.' Sophia was eager to show him her gifts. 'I had no idea that one received presents at one's "Come–Out" . . . it is really most agreeable!'

'Then perhaps you would care to add one more gewgaw to your collection.' He opened a little box and took out a dainty ring set with seed pearls, which he slid expertly on her finger.

'How lovely it is!' she exclaimed. 'And it fits exactly! However did you manage to guess the size?'

He threw Lottie a droll look and said carelessly, 'Oh, it is one of the many skills a gentleman acquires in the course of an eventful life.'

Sophia accepted his explanation with equanimity, and while she admired her ring Prince Paul turned his attention to Lottie once more, only to find her regarding him in a vaguely puzzled way.

'Don't tell me I have succeeded in surprising you, lovely Lottie?' he murmured.

'If so, the surprise is a pleasant one,' she said in her forthright way. 'Naturally I had hoped that you would be generous in your support for Sophia this evening. The child is grown very fond of you.'

'I know. Extraordinary, isn't it?' His mouth quirked in self-mockery. 'Stranger still, I believe I am in serious danger of coming to enjoy her regard.' He saw her frown deepen. 'You don't approve?'

'On the contrary,' she said quietly. 'If I could be sure you meant it, I should be delighted for Sophia. All I ask is that you don't encourage her affections only to let her down when the novelty wears thin.'

'What a very low opinion you have of me,' he drawled, his grey eyes darkening. 'I do occasionally wonder what I must do to please you.'

However, for the next hour or two at least, Lottie could not fault his behaviour. Indeed, in some indefinable way he seemed to take charge of events, and unpredictable as ever, assumed the mantle of authority with consummate ease. He was every inch a Bayersdorf as he stood at the head of the line beside his niece, receiving their guests – his magnificent uniformed figure, and that hint of arrogance in the handsome face – made all the more singular by reason of its distinguishing scar – seeming quite naturally to command both admiration and respect.

As he moved away to lead Sophia into the opening dance, his head so fair and hers so dark, Countess von Deiter observed in her rather carrying voice: 'How fortunate that His Royal Highness consented to honour us this evening, Baroness. There is no denying that the occasion must gain greatly from his being here!'

Pink ostrich plumes nodded importantly in the brassy coiffure that Lottie had more than once uncharitably hazarded owed more to her hairdresser's art than to nature, and the Countess' sharp features mirrored her complacence. This was her finest hour since her husband had become Secretary of State to Prince Adolphus, and she was resolved that it would be but the first of many. It was almost two years now since Otto Raimund's death, yet still everywhere one went it was of him and his beautiful vivacious wife that people spoke. And it was to Lottie Raimund even now that the diplomatic world paid court, rather than the Count, her husband, and it was to Lottie Raimund that Prince Adolphus still turned.

But this evening, protocol had demanded that the von Deiters should take their rightful place with the reception party, and the experience had fired her ambition anew. A brief glance at her husband standing beside her – short of stature, his girth rigidly restrained by corseting, and a manner that veered between vain pomposity and an almost obsequious eagerness to please those above him in rank or cleverness – was enough to confirm to her why he had so far failed to make any appreciable impression upon the diplomatic scene. But much as her ambitious soul might crave an Otto Raimund, the Countess was at heart a realist and her determination to become first lady was in no way impaired by her husband's shortcomings, though it meant dragging him every inch of the way.

Lottie Raimund might give herself airs, but Adolphus was failing fast – recent letters from friends in Gellenstadt had confirmed as much – and without Adolphus to bolster her ego,

Lottie's star would quickly wane. Even her influence over the young Princess would cease once Sophia was married – and Prince Paul would ensure that a husband was wisely chosen!

But for now in the ballroom all was gaiety and light, laughter and music. Alys Annesley was very much aware of the atmosphere, her senses being acutely attuned to every nuance of sound as she sat, her chair half-screened from view by the great perfumed banks of flowers and greenery flanking the dais where the orchestra played.

Max had been loath to leave her there, but she had been adamant, determined that his evening should not be ruined.

'You mustn't worry about me or I shall be wishing I had not come. Lottie has gone to a great deal of trouble to ensure my comfort, and Cousin Carrie is close by with Lady Merrivale if I should need anything, so please, dear Max, go and enjoy yourself. I'm sure Arabella must be impatient, waiting for you to ask her to dance,' she concluded lightly. 'And I have no wish to be blamed for keeping you from her!'

He did not trouble to tell her that Arabella had long since tired of waiting for him and was about to dance the cotillion with a rather gangling young man who, from his dress and the richness of the orders adorning his chest, he deduced to be someone of importance.

Max supposed he ought not to be surprised that Arabella was so much in demand, or indeed that she should be flattered by the attentions being lavished upon her, for she was young and wilful and very beautiful – and though it saddened him a little to see her being so much influenced by Lady Sarah Bingley, his feelings were not sufficiently engaged for him to be hurt by her flightiness, except in his pride, perhaps.

He stood near the door watching as the cotillion progressed, and as the figures moved and fluttered in shimmers of colour he saw Sophia looking very happy with a young man he didn't recognize, and a moment later caught the unmistakable flash of pink – the Baroness was dancing with Alexei Metlin. Jealousy stirred unexpectedly within him as she laughed up at the dashing young Russian. Taking himself severely in hand he concentrated instead upon the quality of the gathering. He had known, of course, that Sophia's ball was likely to be a prestigious affair, but he had not expected quite such a plethora of princes and princesses. There were said to be upwards of thirty minor German royalties represented at the Congress, and it seemed that most of them were here – to say nothing of diplomats and duchesses, counts and courtesans!

'I feel decidedly *de trop* amongst all this gold and silver lace,' he had confessed wryly to Lottie before the commencement of the ball.

'You, my dear sir?' she had said with a trill of laughter, and had stepped back to survey with a critical eye the black inexpressibles, the severe but superbly cut black swallow-tailed coat and the snowy waistcoat. She lingered over his cravat, which was a marvel of complexity with a single diamond pin thrust into its folds, before giving a satisfied nod and saying to Alys in her teasing way, 'You are fortunate, my dear, in having for escort the most elegant man in the room!' Her words echoed now in his ears as the chandeliers made a glittering spectacle of the crowded ballroom.

'Impressive, isn't it?' said a dry quiet voice, and Max turned in some relief to find Lord Castlereagh standing beside him, as soberly garbed as himself. 'Lottie Raimund always did have a flair for this sort of thing. Did you know her husband?'

Max confessed that he had not had that pleasure.

'Splendid fellow. Wasted where he was, of course – in any of the great capitals of the world he'd have risen right to the top.' His lordship sighed. 'We could do with a little of his kind of clear-headedness at this time.'

'Matters are going well enough, though, aren't they?' Max asked.

'Matters are not *going* at all, my dear Annesley, though that, I'm sure I need not tell you, is not something I would have made known to all and sundry.' The cool voice continued: 'All are filled with petty obsessions. The Czar can think only of Poland, and Hardenburg wants Saxony for Prussia and Frederick William. Talleyrand, it sometimes seems to me, wants nothing more than to prevent everyone else from reaching agreement, while Prince Metternich – ' His eyes strayed to the handsome figure of the Austrian Minister who was at that moment performing a graceful *tour de mains*. He concluded, with a glacial smile, ' – is obsessed with keeping us entertained. The Czar calls him the best master of ceremonies in the world, and by God, I'm not sure that he is not right! One can scarcely ever bring him to be serious, except about trivialities!'

'And what does Lord Castlereagh want?' Max asked quietly.

'My dear sir, I just want matters settled with as little fuss as possible,' said his lordship wearily, as his attention was claimed elsewhere.

Across the room, Alexei Metlin was murmuring into Lottie's ear and, from her reaction, it must have been quite a compliment. Max felt like a voyeur and looked quickly away.

'Alexei, I could kiss you!' Lottie exclaimed, and as they parted and came together again, Alexei grinned lasciviously.

'I may hold you to that, *moya dorogoya*!'

'You aren't teasing – the Czar really does mean to come?'

'I have his solemn word. I am to go and fetch him about one hour from now.'

'But how ever did you persuade him to come?'

Alexei chuckled. 'By telling him that Princess Bagratian would be here. He is presently infatuated with her.'

'But I thought that she and Prince Metternich . . .'

'Quite so.' Alexei's eyes gleamed wickedly. 'Only she is madly jealous because he has dared to look elsewhere. Also, my Emperor is at odds with Metternich on quite another score. It is all highly entertaining! Watch and you will see how studiously they avoid one another!'

Lottie laughed. 'You are quite incorrigible! What am I to do if they come to blows in my ballroom?'

'I only wish that I could guarantee you such entertainment, but it will not happen, I fear!' He glanced across the heads of the other dancers. 'The little one is enjoying her ball, I think?'

'Prodigiously. My only fear is that she may be danced off her feet before the night is out!'

'And von Gratz? I see he is here.'

'Yes.' Lottie's glance grew troubled. 'So far he has been the model of discretion. I don't know what Prince Paul said to him the other day, but it seems to have had the required effect, and it is to be hoped that with so many beautiful women to distract him, he will forget about Sophia for tonight at least.'

Lottie was closer to the truth than she knew, though her

hope about Sophia was ill-founded. Duke Franz had not forgotten; he had merely decided to change tactics – and therefore saw no advantage in attempting to woo a tongue-tied, unwilling ingénue in full view of half of Vienna, when the conquest might be accomplished in quite another way.

Be subtle, Paul had said. He had been furious at the time, but since then an idea had begun to formulate in his mind; it would, however, require careful planning – and must not be rushed.

It was during a brief entertainment by members of the ballet that Prince Paul first noticed the young woman sitting a little way apart from everyone else, half concealed by the banks of greenery – and looking so pale and insubstantial in her slim diaphanous gown that he thought at first that he must be imagining her. Curious, he went closer – and wonder became recognition. It was Annesley's sister. She looked very young and there was something desperately vulnerable in her attitude.

Prompted by some quixotic impulse, he made his way towards her. There was no sign of her brother – and many of the seats near to her were unoccupied, the ladies having moved forward for a better view of the performance; inadvertently he kicked one of the little gilt chairs. Only then, when it was too late to draw back, did he notice the glint of tears. Damn!

She was leaning forward in a tense listening attitude.

'Good evening, Miss Annesley,' he said, annoyance with himself making his voice brusque.

She started, a little colour creeping into her pale cheeks, and he saw that she was making a desperate effort to pull herself together.

The voice was vaguely familiar to her, but she could not immediately place it. Nor did she particularly wish for company. She made a brief indecisive gesture. 'I'm sorry . . . you must forgive me. You are . . . ?'

'Paul – Sophia's uncle.'

'Yes, of course.' Whatever could he want with her?

He was beginning to wonder much the same thing. 'Why are you hiding away up here among the dowagers?' he asked abruptly.

Alys gasped, taken aback as before by his abrasive manner,

and then found herself saying shakily, with a brave attempt to be flippant, 'Why does one usually hide, sir?'

'Presumably because one does not wish for company,' he said dryly. 'But if that is the case, why come at all?'

'Why indeed?' Her laugh was a choked little sound, and she swallowed convulsively to steady her voice. 'I thought it might help . . . listening to the music.' How silly it had been to think that just because Herr Graber was playing . . . She shook her head. 'And to please Sophia, perhaps, I don't know. But oh, I wish that I had not come!' This last was a low vehement moan.

Paul was also by now wishing himself anywhere but where he was, and yet something about this girl, her odd youthful dignity, the courage he sensed beneath her present distress, held him there.

'You are clearly not yourself, Miss Annesley,' he said. 'Allow me to find your brother – '

'No!' Alys exclaimed with even greater vehemence. 'I won't have his evening spoiled by my stupidity! My cousin will be back shortly. She went with Lady Merrivale to watch the ballet dancers.' She drew a shuddering breath. 'If I could just collect myself . . .'

The music rose to a crescendo, signifying that the entertainment was drawing to a close. What kind of conclusions would the tabbies leap to on their return – this helpless girl in tears and he standing over her? With his reputation who would believe that he was attempting to succour, not seduce? Paul looked about him, a little desperate now himself – chivalry was a virtue he had seldom practised, yet much as he cursed his situation, he could not leave Miss Annesley exposed to prurient eyes, and she was powerless to help herself.

'There is a small anteroom close by,' he said. 'If you will trust yourself to me, it may afford you a few moments in which to recover your composure.'

Alys lifted her head, trying to gauge his mood. But his voice gave little away. 'Thank you,' she said simply.

The room was unoccupied and Prince Paul led Alys to an ornate little sofa, one of a pair set against the wall. Even here all was gilding and rococo plasterwork, but as the sound receded, at least it was peaceful, and as she sighed and closed her eyes, he found himself abruptly saying: 'Do you want to talk?' His mouth twitched. 'They say confession is good for the soul!'

Alys had been so sure that she could not speak of it to anyone, yet after a moment, the words came tumbling out . . . the true reason for their visit to Vienna, to see the good Dr Strauss whose reputation had reached them in England, and who had with such kindness killed her last vestige of hope.

'After four years I had thought I was resigned. I even convinced myself that nothing would come of this visit. That's why we told no one . . . so that I wouldn't have to endure the pity and sympathy all over again.' Her steady narrative began to falter. 'But now . . . well, it suddenly seems so final. Can you imagine how it feels to know that for the rest of your life you will be dependent on others for even the smallest things?'

From beyond the door came the faint strains of a waltz, but in the little room all was silence. Paul knew that she was awaiting his answer, but his jaw was clenched against an unreasoning anger. He was unsure whether it was directed at her for involving him, or against Providence that had dealt so cruelly with her.

'No,' he said at last, his voice grating in the stillness. 'But I can think of worse fates.'

'Oh!' It was a choked gasp of a sound. 'How . . . callous you make it sound!'

'Do I?' he said. 'Forgive me. I must have misunderstood. Shall I then offer you pity, after all? It would be quite genuine, believe me!'

If she had thought his manner abrasive before, it was as nothing to this! He sounded furious, and yet . . . She found herself being challenged in a way no one had ever attempted before, and painful though she found the experience, it suddenly seemed terribly important to pursue it.

'Please,' she said quietly, gathering her courage, 'do go on. I think a few home truths might be very salutary.' A smile flickered. 'Perhaps I have suffered too long from an excess of kindness.'

The unexpected touch of humour came closer to unmanning him than all her tears. 'My dear girl, you overestimate my fitness to admonish you – let alone offer advice!' he confessed in mocking self-denigration. 'I am the very last person to tell anyone else how to go on!'

'But I want you to,' she reiterated with surprising stubbornness.

Paul frowned, looking down at her as she sat there in her pale jonquil gown, so slim and straight and so damnably vulnerable, her head a little bowed as though she were staring fixedly at her clasped hands. Except that she couldn't see anything. *Can you imagine how it feels?* she had asked him, and his answer came back now to mock him. God. What a hypocrite he was! What a miserable lying hypocrite! He wouldn't be able to endure her fate with one millionth part of this girl's courage! And yet here she was, asking *him* to pontificate! Humility – an emotion with which he was totally unfamiliar – touched him briefly.

'Well, for a start,' he began, his voice for once devoid of mockery, 'since you can't change your state, isn't it time you stopped trying so valiantly to live with your blindness, and set about learning how to enjoy life in spite of it?' Again he heard that tiny gasp of sound, and he almost faltered until her whispered 'Go on,' prompted him to continue. 'You can hardly describe your recent ventures into company as *living*,' he concluded. 'I have been several times in your presence, yet this is the first time I have been really aware of you as a person, for you seem determined always to shrink into the background.'

'Because I'm afraid,' she admitted haltingly.

'Of what? Of people? Or of making a fool of yourself, perhaps?' He put a hand under her chin, lifting it. 'You are lovely, young Alys, in a quite special way, and your hair is like spun silver.' His fingers touched it lightly. 'So stop hiding behind potted palms and give people a chance to know you – even to help you. Perhaps they are afraid, too!'

She drew a quick breath. 'You know, in four years, that has never occurred to me! Oh, thank you!'

Her face was alive now, glowing with hope, and Paul felt an uncomfortable jolt of responsibility. What in pity's name had he started? Still, it was much too late now to turn back. He said abruptly, 'Do you dance?'

'N–no,' she stammered. 'I had lessons, of course, when I . . .

when I was a girl, but now, the sets would be too difficult . . .'

'Well, here beginneth your new lesson.' He took her hands and pulled her to her feet. 'The waltz has no sets, so you don't need to be able to see,' he said, and with one hand placed firmly against her back, he began to guide her slowly round the room to the distant music, apparently oblivious of the tears that streamed unheeded down her cheeks. Gradually, as she responded with more sureness to the pulsating rhythm, he increased the pace. 'There, you see? With a little practice, you should be able to acquit yourself quite admirably!'

The teasing mockery in his voice fell like balm on her ears as half-laughing, half-sobbing, she flung back her head with joy – and he, on impulse bent and just touched his lips to hers.

And that was the moment when Lottie, with Max Annesley at her side, pushed open the door.

6

For a moment no one moved. Then:

'The devil!' Max Annesley strode forward, his face white with rage, while Lottie, with a calmness she was far from feeling, glanced swiftly back to assure herself that no one was watching – and looked straight into Countess von Deiter's eyes.

She flung her a brilliant smile, shut the door unhurriedly and leaned back against it, stifling an overwhelming urge to scream. Something of her intensity of feeling was evident in her voice, which shook very slightly.

'Highness – *how could you*? This is madness! I would not have believed that *even you* could sink so low!'

Had she been less angry, the expression in his eyes might have given Lottie pause; as it was, he neither moved nor spoke, and she had too much else to worry about to notice.

Alys, in the circle of Prince Paul's arm, a trifle pink from being kissed and still in a state of euphoria, did not immediately register what was happening, but she greeted their arrival with pleasure.

'Oh, how splendid! You are just in time to see . . .'

But her brother saw only the tears still wet on her face – and Alys in the arms of this royal dissolute whom he had seen with his own eyes, only moments before, subjecting her to his odious advances. There was but one thought in his head.

Lottie guessed what must be his intention and ran forward to catch at his arm. 'No! Mr Annesley . . . Max, pray don't!'

He brushed her aside with indifference, and had Alys not spoken, he must surely have thrown himself upon the Prince and attempted to choke the life out of him without regard for the consequences. But the sound of his sister's voice, troubled, even a little aggrieved, reached him at last and he turned instead to grasp the hand she held out, drawing her to himself, away from the Prince.

'Max . . . what is it? Why are you so angry? I had thought you would be pleased!'

He uttered something like a groan and said gently, 'My dear, you don't understand.' His eyes, like hard blue chips, belied the gentleness. They moved to Prince Paul and then found Lottie. 'Perhaps, Baroness, you would oblige me by taking Alys away from here.'

'Leaving you and Prince Paul to come to cuffs – or worse?' she cried, incensed beyond all measure. 'Indeed I will not!'

'No, and I will not go anywhere either,' Alys declared, her uncertainty turning to fear, 'until someone tells me *what* is happening!'

The silence that followed was broken by Prince Paul whose eyes held a curious blankness more chilling than mere anger. He said with contemptuous irony, 'My dear Miss Annesley, I infer that your brother in his roundabout way is accusing me of attempting to seduce you and is resolved upon calling me to account.'

'Oh, no!' she exclaimed, turning her head a little towards him. 'But that is *ridiculous* . . .'

In spite of the tenseness of the situation, Lottie found herself momentarily diverted by Paul's reaction to this. He was not accustomed to having his advances, however innocent, so lightly dismissed – and she could have sworn that it put him out of countenance, if only briefly.

'Isn't it, though?' he drawled silkily. 'Highly ridiculous! Would that I had been less noble when the opportunity offered itself!'

Alys blushed, unused to this kind of exchange and uncertain therefore quite how to respond. Lottie groaned inwardly, knowing it to have been deliberately inflammatory – an opinion shared by Max, who put Alys aside and stepped forward with murder in his face.

'You will answer for that, sir!' he snapped.

Prince Paul shrugged. 'If it's satisfaction you crave, I shall be delighted to oblige you.'

Even before Alys had cried 'No, you can't! Lottie, you mustn't let them!' Lottie's patience had snapped.

'Stop it this minute, both of you!' she demanded, and ran between them so that they were each forced to back away. 'I have never heard such childish nonsense! In case you had forgotten, you are both my guests and this is Sophia's Coming

Out ball!' Her voice was low, passionate in its intensity, and her hand shook a little as she gestured towards the door. 'Out there is gathered almost everyone of note in Vienna, and I *will not* have the whole evening set at nought by your stupid brawling! Alys is none the worse for her experience, are you, Alys?'

'No, of course not. Quite the opposite, in fact.'

'You see? It is a fuss about nothing. Sleep on it if you will, and should you wish to make an end of one another, you are at perfect liberty to do so tomorrow, but not here – not now!'

Max Annesley was the first to respond; a little shamefaced, he said stiffly, 'You are quite right, ma'am. Pray accept my apologies and assurance that much as it goes against all inclination, I am willing to sink my differences with His Highness for this evening at least.'

'The devil you are!' murmured the Prince.

Lottie turned on him, her blazing eyes grown almost black with the force of her emotions. 'Don't, Highness, I beseech you, aggravate matters just when we are on the point of resolving them! There is too much at stake.' She drew a deep steadying breath and strove for calm. 'The reason I came in search of you was to tell you that Alexei Metlin has somehow managed to persuade the Czar to look in later this evening, and you must admit that it is the most tremendous accolade – it will set the seal of success upon Sophia's début! But Alexei has already left to bring him, and we must both be ready to greet him when he arrives! You must come with me now.'

Oh, please don't let him be difficult, she found herself pleading silently, as she anxiously watched those handsome brooding features for some sign that he might be on the verge of giving ground. Inconsequentially, she observed how the tautness in his face made the skin around his scar pucker slightly, and combined with that fashionably unruly swirl of tow-coloured hair, it lent him something of the truculence of a small boy resisting coercion, so that for a moment she was prey to the oddest temptation to put up a hand to smooth out the tautness and coax him back into good humour. She pulled herself together swiftly.

'Time is short, sir. If you will not heed me, then I beg you to think of Sophia,' she resumed earnestly in the face of his continuing silence, then, looking him full in the eyes: 'You know how she feels about you – if you fail her now, her disappointment will be such that she may never forgive you for it!' Lottie lifted her head in unconscious challenge. 'And I certainly won't!'

He continued to stare at her, his brows drawn into a frown as he pondered on that strange fleeting softness in the pool-deep blue of her eyes a few moments ago, almost as if . . . Now, there was a thought! But there was no sign of weakness in her present mood, persuasive though it sought to be. Damn you, Lottie Raimund! he cursed her silently, even as a faint wry gleam lit his eyes.

'What can I say, lovely Lottie? You surely know how to stir a man's conscience – to say nothing of his heart!'

Lottie was unsure how to take this. She knew these mercurial changes of old, and when he looked as he did now one could never be sure what was in his mind.

'Does that mean that you *will* come?' she asked directly.

'Why not?' The cynicism in his voice and the almost bruising clasp of his hand on her arm were hardly reassuring. 'Let us by all means prepare a welcome for Alexander, guaranteed to flatter even his inflated ego!'

It was not a promising start, but fearful of provoking him afresh, Lottie allowed herself to be propelled willy-nilly towards the door, with no time to do more than glance back over her shoulder. The Annesleys had not moved. Max, with his arm protectively round Alys, still wore that set look – and she thought there was added to it now a hint of reproach, perhaps even of disappointment in his eyes as they met hers.

She made an irresolute gesture and said impulsively, 'Forgive us . . . and, oh, do please come back to the ball!' and felt a foolish lump form in her throat as he replied gravely: 'Thank you, but I believe Alys may prefer to retire. It has been a rather more . . . eventful evening than she is accustomed to, so if you don't mind . . .'

Lottie wanted to say that she *did* mind, but Prince Paul was before her. With no more than the briefest backward glance he said, with true Bayersdorf austerity: 'Why do you not allow your sister to decide, sir? '

Max Annesley's eyes immediately darkened once more and

Lottie was in despair when to her surprise Alys spoke, an unfamiliar note of resolution in her voice.

'Dearest Max, I'm not in the least tired, truly, and I should very much like to go back to the ballroom if you will take me.'

At this the Prince turned to look at her, releasing his hold on Lottie in order to applaud softly. 'Bravo, Miss Alys!' he said, and Lottie could not recall ever having heard quite that degree of genuine warmth in his voice. It should have reassured her, but instead had the reverse effect. Alys was so vulnerable and he could charm as no other when he so desired.

'And what exactly was all that about, Highness?' she demanded of him, sotto voce, whilst smiling and nodding to people as they passed. 'What happened in there between you and Alys?'

He smiled down at her, a glittering oblique shaft of slate-hard insolence; the *even you* she had uttered so accusingly earlier still rankling. 'That, my dear Lottie, is between me and Miss Annesley, and is none of your business!'

'Oh, how despicable! If you in any way attempted to take advantage of her, I shall *make* it my business!' she hissed furiously through her teeth, quite forgetting in her agitation that she had not meant to aggravate him.

The Prince bowed with exquisite correctness to a lady in puce satin, who was left in a state of nerves, wondering what she had done to merit so witheringly glacial a smile.

'I tremble, *Gnädige* Baroness!' he drawled. 'What will you do, I wonder? Have me run through in some dark alley, or drop a few pertinent words in my brother's ear in the hope that he will disown me?'

'No, of course not!' she spluttered indignantly. 'Don't be ridiculous!' And then, as they arrived at the door, the hostess in her took over once more. 'Oh, heavens, we can't be quarrelling now! The Czar will be arriving at any moment and Sophia must be found! Paul, do go and look for her . . . see, the set is just coming to an end. I must find Josef and make sure that he has arranged for the orchestra to play something suitable during the formal reception.'

She was too preoccupied to notice that in the stress of the moment his name had slipped out, or that before inclining his head ironically and departing to do her bidding, he gave her a particularly penetrating look.

Czar Alexander's visit was later acknowledged by almost everyone to have been a spectacular coup. From the moment of his entry into the ballroom to the triumphal strains of the march from *Judas Maccabeus* – 'See The Conquering Hero Comes' (a choice of music which moved Prince Paul to raise a wildly quizzical eyebrow at Lottie behind the Emperor's back, and momentarily threatened her own composure) he was all magnanimity.

He declared himself quite enchanted by Sophia, who behaved very prettily, but though he lavished compliments upon her, it was towards Lottie that his eyes constantly strayed. And when, the formal reception at an end, he began to circulate among the guests, he let it be known that he wished Lottie to accompany him.

'Have a care, *moya dorogoya*,' Alexei whispered wickedly in her ear. 'I know my Emperor. You may well find yourself being considered as his next conquest!'

'Be silent, wretched man!' she begged him, trying not to laugh.

But the mischief was done; from that moment she became increasingly aware of the partiality of Alexander's attentions. And she was not alone. Several pairs of eyes marked their progress with varying degrees of disapprobation. Countess von Deiter was heard to remark spitefully that it was 'distressing to observe how blatantly *some people* put themselves forward!', whilst the eyes of the Czar's latest amour, Princess Bagration, flashed in a way that convinced the tattlemongers that he would pay dearly for his fickleness later.

Alexander could not, however, be faulted in his punctiliousness. He neglected no one of importance, being in particularly kindly mood while conversing with the courtly and much revered Prince de Ligne, who in his eightieth year was the envy of many a younger man. The only sign of the petulance for which the Czar was known in some quarters came during his brief meeting with Prince Metternich, when each accorded the other the barest of civilities.

It was an awkward moment, but was soon over – and after graciously agreeing to partake of supper, during which he was entertained by the renowned Tyrolean Singers, he finally took his leave, carrying Lottie's hand to his lips with a rather unnerving degree of fervour whilst making a passionate declaration that they would meet again 'very soon'.

Sophia teased her about her conquest, and Alexei rolled his eyes as he departed, but Prince Paul was less amused.

'If you want a piece of advice, stay clear of any involvement there,' he said abruptly. 'It will bring you nothing but trouble.'

'Thank you, Highness,' she said sweetly. 'Should I ever find myself in such desperate straits as might warrant seeking your advice, I will remember.'

He flushed and a muscle twitched at the corner of his mouth. 'Oh, you will do as you please, I know that. But there is such a thing as being too clever! Remember that, too!'

With the departure of the Czar, Lottie felt a great lightening of spirits and determined that she would enjoy what remained of the evening. The Annesleys had already slipped away, Alys finally succumbing to tiredness. Lottie had hoped that Max would return, but he did not, and with no shortage of partners all clamouring for her favour, the disappointment soon faded, and night was dwindling into morning before the last of the guests took their leave.

Only towards the end was her enjoyment marred by the sight of Prince Paul in earnest conversation with von Gratz and Count von Deiter. Even as she watched, they were joined by the King of Bavaria's son-in-law, Prince Eugene Beauharnais, and it was no accident, perhaps, that their glances more than once turned in the direction of the by then less crowded ballroom floor where Sophia, her energy undiminished, was dancing a lively polonaise with Alexei Metlin.

7

Had Lottie attempted to measure the success of Sophia's début in terms of callers, the days that followed, and that first day in particular, must have provided ample proof of its having been little short of a triumph, for it seemed that her salon was destined seldom to be free of visitors.

Lady Merrivale was the first to arrive, bringing with her Arabella.

'Gracious, my dear, how fresh you look! I'm sure I don't know how you contrive to look so blooming when you cannot have been more than an hour or two in your bed. And there was I, fearing that we might be too early for you!'

Lottie's skin did indeed glow with health and her eyes sparkled deep blue against their clear translucent whites as she confessed: 'To tell the truth, I have not been to bed at all. The last guest didn't leave until five, and I was out riding before seven.'

'Well, I'm sure I envy you your stamina! But then, I suppose you must still be up in the throes of exhilaration. Such a success! I cannot remember when I have enjoyed myself more. Your beautiful rooms, the ballet, the singers . . . all quite exceptional. And however did you manage to tempt the Czar? My dear, that was a stroke of genius . . . I said as much to Arabella, did I not, my love? Such a handsome man!'

'I think Prince Paul far more attractive,' said Miss Merrivale with the first glimmer of enthusiasm she had shown since her arrival though Sophia had made several shy efforts to engage her interest. Only when the company had grown considerably and included a certain tall, rather gauche-looking young man did she suddenly become animated.

'Do you know Count Laurien?' her ladyship enquired of Lottie, and it was evident from the gleam in her eyes that this was no casual question. 'Well of course you must, since he was one of your guests! He is Hungarian, is he not?' Her voice sank confidentially lower. 'Very wealthy, I believe! It is quite affecting, don't you think, to see how smitten he is with my Bella – though they had not met before last night!'

Lottie's eyes opened wide. 'But I thought that she and Max Annesley were . . .'

'My dear Charlotte, you know how it is with these young gels . . . Your little Princess will be the same, no doubt . . . always fancying themselves in love with first one and then another!' (As if I were quite beyond the age of any such foolishness! Lottie thought indignantly.) 'For my own part, I should be delighted to have Max for a son-in-law, but I have sometimes wondered recently whether he is not, perhaps, a little too set in his ways for Bella . . . and then there is Alys.' Here her ladyship had the grace to look a trifle uncomfortable. 'It is asking a lot of a young girl, don't you think, to expect her to share her husband with a sister so dependant upon him?'

Lottie could almost hear Arabella voicing the objection, and for a moment she was too indignant to answer. She had not thought Lady Merrivale would be so easily swayed! As she struggled to find words, Arabella's tinkling laugh rang falsely in her ear, and she recalled having heard that same laugh last evening, and the young girl's petulant voice declaring to a friend: 'Lud! I declare that if Max is now going to make a habit of bringing Alys with him to balls, I shall begin to find him exceeding tedious!'

Lady Merrivale eyed her young companion's severe face and was prey to all manner of misgivings. 'You are shocked, I think,' she said with something of her usual bluntness. 'But a mother with daughters to bestow must consider many things. Arabella is a lively gel – a trifle too lively at present, I fear, but that will pass, I am sure. She needs someone who will indulge her flights, in moderation, of course, and Max, charming though he is, and I *am* very fond of him,' she added hastily, 'is not exactly exciting . . .'

Her voice petered out. Lottie was tempted to conclude her peroration for her with the damning '*besides which, a mere heir to an English earldom is nowhere near so dashing as a wealthy Hungarian Count!*' but she crushed the unworthy impulse. There was a strong doubt in her mind whether Count Laurien had anything so permanent as marriage in view, but she guessed that any attempt to voice her doubts would not be kindly received, so she contented herself with something suitably noncommittal.

As if to salve her conscience, Lady Merrivale cast her an arch smile. 'Perhaps, in the end, it could all be for the best, my dear. I doubt Max's feelings for Bella were ever seriously engaged, and I have noticed recently that his interest is straying elsewhere!'

Her meaning was unmistakable. Lottie blushed, the more so as the Annesleys arrived at that very moment, and whilst paying their respects, Max said in a low voice that he would appreciate the favour of a few words with her when it should be convenient. Very conscious of Lady Merrivale's eyes upon her, she promised to be at his disposal as soon as Alys was settled.

'My dear Max, pray let your sister come and bear me company for a while. I should like it of all things!' Lady Merrivale was all graciousness. 'Come, my dear Miss Annesley!' Her ladyship raised her voice, as though Alys were hard of hearing, so that everyone turned momentarily to watch.

Max was visibly annoyed, but where Alys would once have shrunk back, she now merely smiled and said, 'How kind!'

Max said nothing as Lottie led him through into one of the smaller salons, but she could feel his anger on his sister's behalf. She said soothingly: 'It is tiresome, I know, but I'm quite sure that Lady Merrivale would be mortally offended if one accused her of insensitivity.'

'Yes,' he said jerkily and then, meeting her eyes, he gave her a rueful smile. 'I suspect I sometimes feel it more than Alys.'

'Well, that is only to be expected,' she said as they sat down on little bamboo seats amid a riot of pagoda-topped cabinets and other examples of chinoiserie. 'We must always feel the need to protect those we love.'

'Yes, well, Alys has decided that she is *over*-protected and means to do something about it.'

Lottie just stopped herself saying 'Good!' There was something in his expression that warned her it would not be well received. Instead she amended it to say with a certain diffidence, 'Might that not be a good thing?'

'Yes, of course. The thing is –' He stood up and began to

prowl the small room. 'The idea seems to have been put into her head by that . . . by Prince Paul.' He stopped and swung round, glaring at her as though she were personally responsible. 'Alys tells me I have grossly misjudged the man, that he was kindness itself, and that I owe him an apology, if you please!' Max frowned. 'That does not sit well with me, and in any case, I am not convinced that his motives were as pure as she imagines! If we had not entered that room when we did . . . her tears . . .'

'Oh, come!' Lottie said, not quite knowing why she was standing up for Paul. 'Alys isn't a fool! We cry for all kinds of reasons, and she didn't look unhappy. Rather the reverse, I thought. I'm sure that what we witnessed was one of those spontaneous and quite harmless little romantic interludes such as any girl of Alys' age dreams about – just because she is deprived of her sight, dear sir, why should she be deprived also of those delicious follies of youth we all secretly hope will come our way?'

Max was momentarily diverted. 'Did you ever long to be kissed by some roué in that hole and corner fashion?'

Oh, how outraged Prince Paul would be to hear himself described as a roué! A gurgle of laughter escaped her. 'But of course! Only in my case, the temptation never presented itself. I was married at seventeen.' He looked as though he was about to start asking awkward questions. 'But to return to Alys, sir, might not the whole experience have been . . . beneficial?'

'If I am to believe all she says, it was positively salutary and seems destined to become the mainspring of her emancipation,' he said dryly.

'Goodness! I had no idea Prince Paul was capable of so much!'

Max sat down again, close to Lottie, still troubled. 'It seems that she confided in him – God knows why, for she insists that he didn't encourage her confidence.' He hesitated, then said harshly, 'You may as well know it all. If he knows, why should not you?' Max explained about the visit to Dr Strauss. 'We both decided it was worth a try. No one else knew, not even our cousin; for all her good qualities, she is not quite the soul of discretion.'

Lottie smiled. 'No.'

'And the Congress made an excellent cover for our visit to Vienna. However, we saw Dr Strauss last Wednesday . . . a charming man and very thorough – '

'But he could do nothing,' Lottie finished for him. 'So that was it.'

Max shrugged. 'I hadn't expected Alys to take the verdict so hard. We both knew that the chances were slight . . . well, nonexistent, really. But Alys took it very strangely.'

'She was certainly very quiet. And you say that Prince Paul played the Samaritan?' It didn't sound at all like him. She tried and quite failed to see him in the rôle of confidant and adviser. 'I wonder what he can have said?'

'As far as I can make out – ' Max sounded aggrieved '– he told her to stop feeling sorry for herself!'

Lottie choked on a laugh. 'Oh, yes, that would fit!'

'Well, whatever it was, it has fired Alys with the determination to enter into things more. I am to practise dancing with her, if you please, though how that is to be accomplished since Cousin Carrie can't play a note . . .'

'Sophia could play for you,' Lottie offered, then a much more interesting idea suggested itself. 'Or, better still, why don't you ask that charming Herr Graber from upstairs? I have been debating whether or not to ask him to give Sophia a few lessons on the pianoforte.'

Max seemed much struck by this, and Lottie stifled a momentary feeling of guilt by reflecting how much pleasure Alys would derive from Ferdie Graber's presence. She was surely entitled to any small indulgence that offered, and besides, it might take her mind off Prince Paul.

'Don't mistake me,' Max was saying. 'No one would be more delighted than I if Alys were to enter more into things. You cannot possibly know how much it would mean to me!'

Lottie was again moved by the intensity of feeling in his voice, and marvelled that Arabella could prefer that over-hearty, chinless young Lothario to someone as caring as Max Annesley. And once one got beyond that initial reserve . . .

She said encouragingly, 'Well, of course I can. It must be clear to anyone who knows you both that you each wish only for the other to be happy!' She stood up. 'And now, I really must get back to my duties.'

'Yes, of course.'

Tasha, who had followed them in and had divided her attentions impartially between them throughout, now became more animated, her tail wagging in expectation of an outing.

Max surveyed her antics with mock severity. 'I have a bone to pick with you, my girl.'

Not fooled for one minute by this admonition, Tasha panted eagerly up at him, sniffing with interest at the finger pointed accusingly.

'That flea-bitten mongrel you have enmeshed in your toils seems to have formed an equally strong attachment for my sister. In fact, it would not be an exaggeration to say that he has appointed himself her sole guide and protector, and now follows her everywhere – even trots behind the carriage when we drive out!'

Lottie laughed. 'Oh no! And is he really flea-ridden?'

He gave her a droll look. 'I have not the slightest doubt of it. Thank God, the creature has not yet taken to following Alys up the stairs! He simply lies in wait on the basement steps.'

'Does Alys mind?

'That's the devil of it.' He grinned suddenly. 'She is almost as besotted as he is!'

Lottie was still laughing as they strolled back into the salon where a great number of people, or so it seemed, had gathered in their absence. Near the window the pale winter sunlight filtered in and came to rest on a familiar flaxen head bent solicitously to an even fairer one.

'Smooth devil!' she heard Max mutter as Prince Paul paused in his absorbing conversation with Alys to mark their return, but a few minutes later she saw the two men exchanging civilities. How different they were, she thought – Max, quietly elegant in his dove grey cutaway coat, and Prince Paul, a touch flamboyant but with that careless grace that was so unsettling.

Lottie dragged her eyes away from them and began to move among the rest of her visitors. Soon she found herself surrounded, and the butt of much gentle raillery from gentlemen who confessed themselves outraged that she should favour one more than the rest to the extent of wishing to be private with him. It was all very lighthearted and gratifying, and soon her cheeks were quite pink and her eyes sparkled.

But she did not, in the midst of it all, forget Sophia. She found her at last at the centre of a group of mostly younger people, among whom were Arabella Merrivale and her Count, the Count's sister, Alexei Metlin and Lady Sarah Bingley, and – her heart sank a little – von Gratz.

'Do not concern yourself, *moya dorogoya*.' Alexei's voice was quietly reassuring at her side. 'Duke Franz is behaving with the utmost propriety.'

And it was true. It was as though he was making a conscious effort to erase the memory of his earlier unfortunate behaviour; to suppress that latent carnality which had so alarmed Sophia at the picnic, and which Lottie herself had been only too conscious of whenever he chose to exert it in her presence.

Now, however, with the exception of an occasional exchange of glances with Lady Sarah, he was in jovial mood and though his teasing was a trifle heavy-handed, the Princess seemed much more at ease with him. Lottie ought to have been reassured; instead she felt a vague prickling of unease.

But there was little time in which to brood. As the remorseless round of pleasure gathered momentum, Lottie had other matters to occupy her mind, not least of which was the embarrassing persistence of Czar Alexander. Her blithe expectation that his interest would wane as swiftly as it had arisen was dashed less than two days later when, during a similar gathering of friends, a small package was delivered bearing her name.

All unsuspecting, she opened it there and then. It contained an exquisite gold hair ornament fashioned in the form of a spray of violets – each flower petal a sapphire of such glowing depths of colour that a gasp of sound rippled round the room – the more curious pressed forward for a better look, eager to know from whom it had come. This at least Lottie could not deny them.

But as Sophia took the little jewel case from her unresisting fingers, she retained sufficient presence of mind to snatch up the accompanying card. 'My small token of thanks for an evening of enchantment,' it read. 'No jewel can ever match the incomparable brilliance of your eyes. Grant me, I beg of you, the privilege of losing myself once more in their beauty very soon.' The swirling signature was unmistakable, but hardly necessary in the circumstances.

'Oh no!' Lottie breathed, turning bright pink and tucking the card quickly into the briefly cut bodice of her dress. She had hoped her gesture would pass unnoticed in all the excitement, but upon looking up she encountered Prince Paul's eyes fixed upon her with sardonic interest.

Alexei chuckled. 'What did I tell you?'

'Did you know about this?' she demanded in soft-voiced accusation.

'Hand on heart! Not an inkling. But I cannot pretend I am surprised.' His eyes twinkled. 'What would you do?'

'Send it back, of course.'

'Oh, but you can't!' Sophia cried. 'It is so very beautiful.' As others joined in with a variety of suggestions, some of them making her blush anew, the Princess sought out her uncle who had said nothing. 'Uncle Paul. Would it not be a wicked shame if Baroness Lottie were to send back so lovely a gift?'

He watched Lottie from beneath lazy eyelids, his expression unreadable. 'That rather depends upon how far she is prepared to go in order to keep it,' he said softly and watched the effect of his words with some interest.

Lottie wanted to strike out at him. No one else had quite his power to rouse her to violence, with the possible exception of his mother. She swallowed her fury and smiled, holding out a hand for the ornament.

'Enough!' she said. 'Give it to me, please, Your Highness. I cannot possible decide anything now.' And she put it away in the top drawer of a handsome japanned cabinet.

Under cover of the conversation, Max Annesley said quietly: 'Shall you send it back?'

She looked steadfastly back at him. 'Would you think badly of me if I did not?'

'Not badly,' he said. 'But I would be a little disappointed, I think.'

It seemed that day as though people would never leave, but eventually the doors closed on the last visitor and Sophia declared herself worn out and went off to rest.

Lottie sat for a few moments with her eyes closed, trying to empty her mind of thought. Then she stood up and went once more to the cabinet. Taking the ornament across to the window, she turned it this way and that so that it caught the light. It really was quite exceptionally beautiful, she mused and alas, much, *much* too expensive to keep. If this was the kind of gift Alexander considered appropriate for someone he hardly knew, then what, she wondered, did he lavish on his acknowledged mistresses? Or could it be, she concluded with wry humour, that as a lure he might well consider it a worthwhile investment?

'For shame!' a familiar, mocking voice reproved her.

'What?' She spun round to see Prince Paul leaning in his careless way against the closed door. How silently he could move when it suited him!

'Did no one ever tell you that covetousness is a bad sin?'

'I'm not – ' She stopped, biting back her indignation. He shouldn't have that satisfaction. 'I thought you had left with the others.'

'I forgot my cane,' he said apologetically.

'Oh, what a *shame*!' she said witheringly, her glance shifting. 'But you have it now, I see.'

'Yes.' He gave it a twirl and set it down on a nearby table. 'It was in the hall. However, having come back I thought – well, it does rather limit one's conversation, having so many people about. Don't you find it so?'

'No.' She looked him in the eye. 'I wasn't aware that we had anything to talk about that couldn't be said in front of friends.'

He covered the ground between them without once taking his eyes from hers, managing to avoid the furniture scattered in his path as if by instinct. Tasha barked, dutifully, then backed away from those purposeful advancing feet.

'I thought we might discuss gifts, and the nature of their interchange,' he said softly.

Lottie had instinctively closed her fingers round the spray and tucked it half behind her back, but he had noted the gesture and without asking leave reached for her hand and, meeting resistance, forced it upward until it came to rest uppermost on his, still clenched. With a shrug she uncurled her fingers, and the spray lay on her palm, each sapphire petal glowing with rich colour. He took it between finger and thumb and held it up critically to the light.

'A pretty bauble,' he acknowledged, and then swiftly, so swiftly that she had no time to dissemble, his eyes locked again with hers. 'From an Emperor's casket, mayhap designed to tempt?'

'You may guess all you like, Highness,' she retorted with more calm than she was feeling. 'I don't propose to discuss my private affairs with you.'

'An unfortunate choice of word, lovely Lottie,' he drawled, 'or maybe a peculiarly apt one?' His glance moved unhurriedly to the neck of her gown, and looking down, she saw with dismay the tiny corner of white pasteboard just visible against the swell of her breast. With awful certainty she read his intention. Her pulse began to beat crazily. He wouldn't! Even Paul wouldn't attempt to . . .

'*Don't you dare*!'

It was a mistake; she knew it even before the words were out, breathy and almost inaudible.

'Dear Lottie! You know I can't resist a challenge!'

Instinctively she stepped back and immediately wished that she had not, for she found herself entangled in the heavy curtains which gave at her touch. With both hands clutching despairingly at the thick velvet folds she was swaying helplessly, and with her feet and the lower part of her legs brought up hard against the window seat, she was quite unable to regain her balance.

A gentleman, she raged inwardly as his cool fingers lingered far longer than was necessary against the warm softness of her flesh before extracting the card, would not have taken advantage of her predicament in that odious way. Nor would he have kept her so ignominiously at a disadvantage while he read the wretched thing!

'I don't care much for Alexander's style,' he mused critically, seemingly unaware of her acute discomfort. 'Too florid by half! But the message is clear enough. I think you had better let me return this trinket for you – less embarrassing for all concerned, and there'll be far less chance of his *importuning* you in the future.'

'You will do nothing of the kind!' Lottie ground the words out.

The Prince looked vaguely surprised. 'You surely don't want a liaison with a man like that?'

'What I *want* is for you to give me back my present and *go away*!'

The muscles in her arms were beginning to ache abominably. Unable to move her feet any further back, she tried to take a fresh grip on the curtain in the hope of pushing herself upright. The outcome was little short of disastrous; with a kind of terrible inevitability, she hung perilously upright for a moment and then swayed forward.

The Prince caught her with commendable agility, and showed no immediate inclination to release her. His face was very close and she could see the glinting devils in his eyes.

'Women are such contrary creatures!' he murmured.

'It was an accident!' she muttered through her teeth, by now very close to tears of rage and exasperation, but grimly holding on to her temper. 'I know you hope I will struggle and make a scene, but I'm not going to.'

'Very sensible,' he approved. 'You aren't afraid that someone might come in?'

'No.' It was blatantly a lie, but she persevered. 'If they do, it will be for you to explain what you are about!'

'Or alternatively,' he said, pulling her close, 'I could make it so abundantly plain that they will be in no doubt.'

Before she could protest, his mouth was on hers, and against all reason she found her resistance spinning away into heights and depths of exquisite sensation that she had not dreamed were possible.

It wasn't like the last time – no gentle questing now, but a deep passionate urge to possess, that demanded and cajoled and exalted by turn, until all her anger at his using her so was drowned out by a greater need for the moment to go on . . . and on . . . And when it was over at last she was left, bereft and shaking, while his fingers, feather-light, traced the trembling contours of her mouth, setting her skin on fire and dragging from her small incoherent sounds. Looking up, she found his eyes no longer grey but black, fixed upon her with an almost feverish intensity.

'Well now, Lottie Raimund, what a surprise you're turning out to be!' His voice sounded oddly husky. 'I'll wager you don't kiss your prim Englishman like that!'

'I don't . . .' The shaking that seemed to fill her body made coherent speech difficult. Lottie cleared her throat and began again, determined to master her disordered senses. 'Mr Annesley has *never* . . . he is a gentleman and would never presume to use me so!'

Paul's mouth curled at the corner. 'Then I grieve for him,' he drawled, mockingly unrepentant. 'Fortunately I am not cursed with any such handicap!'

'No! *Oh, would that you were!*'

It was a cry from the heart and as such, had a curious effect on him, rousing in him an unfamiliar desire to protect her. Not that she was in need of protection, for although her voice was still stifled, she was already much more in command of herself. With a twinge of regret he judged it time to release her. As he did so, she winced and he realized that he still held the Czar's trinket in his hand. The sapphire petals must all this time have been painfully embedded in the small of her back. A fleeting smile crossed his face. Did she have the least idea, he wondered, just how it betrayed the extent of her emotions that she had not been aware of it until that moment?

Lottie misunderstood the smile. It seemed to reduce what had been for her an earth-shaking experience to the level of trivial dalliance. And she cursed herself for a fool. How pliant she had been! How naive! And how mortified she now was! Small wonder that he smiled. Her only hope must be that he did not retail so amusing an experience to his friends.

Lottie gathered the shreds of her dignity. 'May I have the Czar's gift to me, if you please – and his note, before you leave?'

That had wiped the smile off his face! She felt marginally better.

The Prince stared down at her for a moment. Then: 'As you will, Baroness.' He put it into her outstretched hand, took the card from his pocket and laid it on top with exaggerated care. Having done so, he bowed formally and turned to go.

'Highness?'

He glanced back. She was poised, calm – much more

beautiful than he had ever seen her – and completely in charge of her emotions once more.

'Don't forget your cane,' she said.

8

'Why is it, Baroness, that you dislike me so?'

The music was liltingly romantic, the Imperial Riding School, transformed by miles of shimmering white silk and silver fringing for one of Emperor Francis' grand routs, was thronged with kings and princes and brilliantly colourful dignitaries of every degree – and through the delicate *mousseline-de-soie* of Lottie's gown, the warm hand of Duke von Gratz pressed with possessive sureness against her back as they circled the floor.

It was an incongruous moment to choose for such a question. Lottie was tempted to prevaricate, to protest that now was not the time, but the bold complaisance of his manner irritated her – as though, she concluded indignantly, she were some poor misguided female who had to be humoured.

'I cannot imagine that my disliking, or for that matter, liking you can be of any great importance, sir,' she replied, her voice pleasant but firm. 'But I do have certain responsibilities concerning Princess Sophia and I take them very seriously.'

'Ah.' She felt a slight stiffening in his manner. 'So?'

'Her Royal highness is very young and inexperienced. Until Vienna she has known very few men except her father – '

'And Paul, surely?' The words were clipped.

'Not even Prince Paul,' Lottie insisted quietly. 'She has been very much in awe of him until recently.' She looked the Duke straight in the eyes and managed not to flinch at the hardness she saw there. 'I would venture to suggest that Sophia is not for you, sir.'

'Would you, indeed, Baroness?' The pressure of his hand on her back increased perceptibly. 'But then, the decision is not for you to make.'

Lottie looked across to where Sophia was dancing with a pleasant, rather shy young man, a cousin of the Esterhazys, in whom she had begun to show some interest of late. Duke Franz followed her glance, and his mouth tightened.

'However,' Lottie said, 'I believe that Prince Adolphus will heed my opinion.'

There was an uncomfortable moment when she felt the fury emanating from him as an almost physical force. Then the music swelled to a crescendo and he whirled her round ever faster and his voice was soft in her ear. 'Opinions can be changed, *Gnädige* Baroness. Mine, also, perhaps, if you have a mind to try? Princess Sophia could well find me the most undemanding of husbands were I to be assured of adequate fulfilment elsewhere!'

His meaning was unmistakable, and Lottie felt herself growing hot, a condition not improved as Prince Paul's face swam momentarily into her line of vision, his expression one of frowning intensity.

'I'm sorry,' she reiterated. 'I have said all I wish to say.'

'Then you must also abide by the consequences,' said von Gratz with ominous calm.

Lottie did her best to put the conversation out of her mind, and in such surroundings this was not difficult to accomplish. For sheer extravagance, the Hofburg *en fête* would be almost impossible to surpass. On this, Sophia's first visit to the Imperial Palace, she had been almost totally robbed of speech.

'Are they real?' had been her whispered utterance when she found the approach to the principal drawing rooms lined on both sides by a complete avenue of orange trees, between each of which was concealed an immense candelabra whose lighted tapers and lustres and crystal drops shed a magical light amid the foliage, throwing into relief the blossoming branches. Here too there were hangings of white silk to set off the huge baskets of flowers and rare plants – and all combined to set the scene for a continuing vista of colour and light, with music wafting on perfumed air.

Even later, when Lottie teased her about Count Enghein, her latest beau, Sophia was still dreamy-eyed. Only when von Gratz claimed a dance did she return looking a little distrait.

Lottie wrote almost weekly to Prince Adolphus so that he should not feel forgotten, mostly of Sophia's many forays into society, of Count Enghein and other young men who sighed after her . . . but all of them, alas, woefully inexperienced in terms of what would be expected of the man Sophia must eventually marry. If only Adolphus were not obsessed with this desire to rush matters! Her heart hollowed as she pondered the reasoning behind it, and even as she willed him to be wrong, the sight of his writing growing more shaky every week seemed to prove him right.

And yet, after the evening at the Hofburg, she had felt compelled to write, warning him about Duke Franz.

On the face of it, dear sire, he must seem an ideal suitor in terms of age and experience, but should you receive from him, as I believe you may, an offer for Sophia's hand, I do beg you will refuse him – not simply because Sophia holds him in great aversion, though that must surely be a consideration – but because I very much fear that if he marries Sophia he will, at the first opportunity, conspire to hand over Gellenstadt to Bavaria, abetted by Count von Deiter and perhaps even your brother.

She almost left the part about Prince Paul out of the letter, but hardened her heart. It was true, and anything that might save Sophia from von Gratz must be used. She continued:

Such a merger would be all too easy to achieve. There seems little immediate prospect of Congress agreeing a satisfactory constitution for the German states, so the King of Bavaria would be only too happy to contemplate the acquisition of more territory if the opportunity should arise. One begins to wonder if matters here will ever be resolved. A Federal Diet with Prussia and Austria at the head has already been rejected by the smaller states as it would have severely curtailed their independent sovereignty, and other proposals have foundered on similar grounds. Your friend, the Duke of Baden, has raised the strongest objections – and Wurtenburg is proving even more obstinate. It now seems certain that sittings will be suspended for a while, to allow tempers to cool.

I have no idea how long you will be happy for us to remain in Vienna, dear sire. With so many matters as yet unresolved, the Congress is clearly destined to last much longer than we had anticipated. Indeed, if the present lack of urgency persists, it could continue indefinitely. His Highness, the Prince de Ligne remarked some weeks ago 'The Congress doesn't march – it dances', and how right he is being proved!

Duke von Gratz's formal offer for Sophia's hand arrived at the

Schloss Bayersdorf one day after Lottie's letter, but Prince Adolphus had scarcely time to think about it before his mother was upon him; Countess von Deiter had taken it upon herself to inform Her Serene Highness of the Duke's intentions.

'You will naturally accept,' the Dowager Princess said, no trace of a doubt in her voice.

The Prince studied his mother's hard unyielding face with a kind of detached curiosity. He had long ago searched for some evidence of kindness or warmth in her, before concluding that in her philosophy kindness would merely equal weakness.

'You would be happy to see your grand-daughter married to that man?'

She looked faintly surprised. 'I fail to see what my happiness has to do with it. You consider it expedient that a husband should be found for Sophia – quite rightly in my opinion. The sooner she is removed from Baroness Raimund's charge, the better pleased I shall be.'

'Mother,' he said wearily, 'could we please *not* go through all that again?'

But Her Serene Highness would not be stopped. She flourished Countess von Deiter's letter with cold triumph. 'Read that and see if I am not justified!' And, as the Prince brushed it aside in distaste, 'Your paragon, Adolphus, is behaving in exactly the kind of bourgeois way I expected she would. Not content with frequenting the wine gardens at Grinzing with officers of the Czar's Imperial Guard – and we all know what breed of young man Alexander attracts to his service – '

'Mother!'

'Not content with that, I say, she has the effrontery to take your daughter picnicking in the woods with those same officers. And now, if you please, she is flirting quite openly with the Czar himself! Irena says that the whole of Vienna is talking about them –'

'Enough!'

Prince Adolphus had begun pacing about the throne room, using up precious energy, precious breath. Now he swung round, cold rage blazing in his eyes. 'For the last time, I will not listen to the seditious tattlemongering of Irena von Deiter! She is as obsessively unreasoning as you are about Charlotte.'

The stood outfacing one another, glances locked, stiff with

pride and obduracy and controlled anger. The only sound in the room was the Prince's ragged, shallow breathing. His mother made a gesture of negation.

'Very well. Let us return to Sophia's betrothal. Duke von Gratz would seem to be an admirable choice.'

'Even though he is known to be licentious, unscrupulous and hungry for power?'

The Dowager Princess rapped the floor with her stick. 'There are always stories about such men. Only the mediocre pass unnoticed! Sophia can only benefit from a union with someone sufficiently strong and mature to command her respect and obedience now, and who has the necessary qualities to rule at her side when the time comes. Besides which,' she concluded harshly, 'he is your brother's friend.'

'That is hardly a recommendation,' Adolphus gasped, seized by a fit of coughing. As he waited for it to subside, his fingers unconsciously curled round Charlotte's letter, crushing it. Devil take Paul! His hand was behind this. *His friend* von Gratz laying claim to Sophia's hand, to Sophia's inheritance ... 'As for Sophia,' he continued painfully, 'she dislikes the Duke. To put it more strongly ... she cannot bear him near her.'

'Pah!' his mother exclaimed. 'I hope you will not heed the megrims of a silly girl! Sophia will do as she is told. If she had not been exposed to unsettling influences, I doubt that such a thought would have entered her head.'

'But it would have entered mine, Mother,' Prince Adolphus said quietly. 'You see, I dislike von Gratz also. I always have.'

9

'My dear, I have been very lax,' Lottie confessed to Sophia. 'Your father charged me most particularly to commission a portrait of you. He wished to hang it in the throne room alongside his own.'

In an attempt to repair this omission she asked Alexei to accompany her one evening to the studios of Isabey near the Café Jungling, only to discover that many of the fashionable were also clamouring for the services of the famous artist.

'Naturally, I shall be delighted to paint the Crown Princess Sophia's portrait,' gushed the one-time disciple of the great David. Lottie thought him a little condescending as he flung out an arm to encompass the many canvases in various stages of completion. 'You can see my difficulty, however. And then, so much of my time each day is spent at the Palace of Schönbrunn, where I am charged by His Majesty, the Emperor, with the task of committing to canvas his grandson, the little King of Rome – the son of Napoleon, you know. Also, I await almost hourly a call to record for posterity the great Congress leaders. And so?' He shrugged.

Lottie thanked him with scrupulous politeness, said she wouldn't dream of adding to his difficulties, and left.

'Poor fellow,' Alexei chuckled. 'He looked positively bewildered. I don't suppose anyone has ever turned *him* down – not since he became the *dernier cri* anyway!' He gave Lottie a droll look. 'What will you do?'

'Commission that talented young man from upstairs, of course,' Lottie said. 'It is what I should have done in the first place. Those sketches he made on the night of the ball were most impressive. If he can paint half as well, he should be encouraged.'

She passed a message to him by way of Ferdie Graber who now came on three mornings a week to tutor Sophia, and the young man, whose name was Eugene, responded with a promptness that spoke more clearly than words of his ambition to succeed.

'I must tell you, *Gnädige* Baroness, that I am no David or even an Isabey,' he confessed with an engaging frankness. 'But if you would care to see some of my paintings?'

He was about to bring them down for her to view, but when Lottie owned to a burning desire to see his studio, he bowed graciously and vowed that he would be honoured to receive her.

'Goodness, you get quite the best view from up here!' she exclaimed, looking out across the rooftops to the distant Wienerwald. 'It must surely inspire you.'

Eugene grinned. 'It is a help, assuredly, but nothing inspires one so much as the necessity to eat.'

Lottie smiled, glancing round the room with its clutter of paints and canvas and clothes, and loving everything about it. And, since his paintings impressed her quite as much as his sketches, she commissioned him on the spot. It was arranged that he would come down with Ferdie to make some informal sketches of Sophia before starting on the actual portrait, and since Alys was present more often than not, an atmosphere of friendly camaraderie soon developed.

'They are such agreeable young men,' Lottie confided to Max. 'And young talent should be encouraged, don't you think?'

He agreed. 'Herr Graber has certainly been most helpful to us. He is an excellent musician, and never seems to begrudge the time he spends playing for Alys so that she may practise her dancing. I must say she has come on remarkably.'

Lottie wondered whether he realized how much of Alys' time was passed in Ferdie's company. If so, he apparently saw no harm in it, and indeed, if the association were to be judged on the amount of laughter issuing from the music room when the four young people were present, it must surely be considered innocent.

But Fräulein Lanner most certainly did not approve. She had protested vehemently that such casual intimacy was not seemly, but the Baroness had seen fit yet again to disregard her advice. After all, she had argued, there could be no possibility of indiscretion if the Fräulein was present at all times. All the repressions of a nature starved of even the most commonplace attentions from any man rose like gall in her throat as she sat in rigid disapproval, only too aware that if the young men noticed her at all, it was with a kind of amused tolerance bordering on pity. Once she caught the painter observing her with a calculating eye. She suspected that he was sketching her, and just for an instant a wild ungovernable fury swept through her; two angry red spots burned on her cheeks, and he, his sheepish grin fading, shrugged and turned away. Such a situation, she vowed, must not be allowed to continue.

So it was that Countess von Deiter came to call; prompted by the Fräulein, she arrived one morning well before the accepted hour, and was witness to a particularly lively session. She stood for a few moments, uninvited, in the open doorway of the music room, observing the scene; Sophia and Alys were seated at the pianoforte with Herr Graber at their backs. Occasionally, he would lean down between them with considerable familiarity to demonstrate some part of the music. 'No, no – not like this, young ladies, but like this!' and his fingers would ripple over the keys with magical expertise. In a chair close by, another young man lounged with an equal lack of formality, sketching furiously and throwing in the occasional witty comment which sent the girls into whoops of laughter.

The Countess exchanged a meaningful glance with Fräulein Lanner before turning away to confront Lottie. 'I am surprised, Baroness,' she said, her voice sharp as ever, 'or perhaps it would be more accurate to say *shocked* to see our Princess in such company.'

'Indeed? I cannot think why, ma'am.' Lottie kept her voice polite. 'It is all perfectly harmless. In fact, I consider these morning sessions to be a most instructive part of Sophia's education – of more use to her than a dozen formal balls, for she is learning how ordinary people go on. It will prove invaluable to her when she comes to take her place as head of state.'

But the Countess went away, cold-eyed.

'I expect a highly coloured account is even now winging its way to Gellenstadt,' Lottie told Alexei a little pensively.

'Poor Lottie! How difficult a time you are having. It comes of having too generous a nature. You want to make everyone happy – your Prince Adolphus, little Sophia, Alys – also those nice young men!' He grinned sympathetically. 'Even with my Emperor you are too kind. Does he still pursue you?'

It was a vexed question. 'I have done all I can to discourage him short of outright rudeness. One can hardly cut so prestigious a monarch, can one?'

'You will have to get yourself a husband, *moya dorogoya*,' he teased her. 'Someone who will guard you jealously from such unwelcome attentions. I would offer myself to you, but I fear I would prove a sad disappointment. To be faithful . . . even to you . . .' He gave a comical little shrug.

The face whose image flashed into Lottie's mind was even more unsuitable (and unwanted, she told herself sternly), but an embarrassed blush suffused her cheeks.

'Oh-ho! I have stumbled on a secret, *hein*?' he chuckled. 'There is someone –' She shook her head vigorously and told him not to be silly. ' – but you do not wish me to know. Ah well!'

Lottie had not seen Prince Paul alone since their last eventful encounter and she had no wish to do so, she reminded herself, angry at the way her thoughts kept turning to him. She saw him often, of course, in the company of an exceedingly beautiful brunette with an impressive title and very few morals, who was exactly right for him!

The Czar was a rather different problem. Lottie had returned his present with a letter expressing her deep gratitude for his generous thought of her, but explaining that so beautiful and extravagant a gesture was much more than she could accept.

By return had come a tiny heart-shaped pin, also of sapphires, with the plea that 'this trifling *bibelot* will be more acceptable, dear Baroness' and an added expectation that they would meet at the Beethoven concert. Since this was a special gala concert, to be given in the presence of the Czar and King Frederick William of Prussia, at which the Great Man was himself to conduct a new work – and Ferdie had particularly wished them to go as he was to be playing in the orchestra – it had seemed prudent to accept the gift and hope that it would be the end of the matter.

But alas, it was not. Her refusal to encourage him merely

whetted Alexander's appetite. He was unaccustomed to meet with opposition, however virtuous the lady in question. At every function he sought her out – *billets-doux* arrived with monotonous regularity, and though Lottie behaved with absolute discretion, the Czar's *tendre* for her could hardly escape the notice of those about them; Prince Metternich in particular took a delight in marking the progress, or lack of it, of Alexander's suit.

Christmas came and went with midnight mass in St Stefan's Cathedral and much exchanging of presents, amongst which was a huge box of sweetmeats from the Czar, cunningly addressed to both Lottie and the Princess. The festivities were marred only a little for his friends by the death in December of the much beloved Prince de Ligne. Though in his eightieth year he had retained the elegant and sprightly air of a much younger man to the very last and had succumbed finally to a chill.

'Poor fellow,' remarked Alexei with a wry twinkle. 'I am told that he took the chill waiting on a street corner for an assignation! Would that I may be as full of optimism when I reach so venerable an age!'

There were to be so many New Year celebrations that people were spoilt for choice. The Baroness and Sophia had of course been invited to the Hofburg to be part of the Emperor's grand festivities, but when the subject was broached, Sophia seemed oddly reluctant.

'You haven't quarrelled with that nice young man, have you?' Lottie enquired casually.

'No, of course not.' But Sophia was still subdued. 'I am just a little tired, I think,' she said evasively, and when Lottie's eyes registered disbelief, she added in a little rush, 'besides, Duke Franz will most probably be there, and – '

'And you don't wish to spoil your evening by subjecting yourself to his unwelcome attentions! My dear child, why didn't you say so? I don't blame you in the least.' Lottie kept her voice cheerfully practical. 'How would it be if we went to Lady Merrivale's? She is giving quite a small party for some of the English people here. I know that is where the Annesleys intend to go.'

'Oh, could we really? The Emperor would not be offended?'

Lottie affected not to notice the look of profound relief that flooded the young girl's face. 'I'm sure we can manage something without giving offence.' She gave a wry chuckle. 'To be honest, I would as lief not have to fend off the Czar, either! So you see, we are both in the same difficulty.'

Their apologies, couched in the most tactful and persuasive terms, were graciously accepted by the Emperor, and the evening turned out to be one of the happiest and, in the end, the most eventful that Lottie could remember.

It was a very special occasion, also, for Alys. She had vowed to begin the New Year in a positive way, by dancing the first waltz after midnight with Max – the first time she had done so in public, for although she now mingled much more, and had made many friends, it had taken until now for her to pluck up the courage to expose herself to so much attention.

The secret had been well kept, even from Mrs Osmond. She was in the middle of a comfortable exchange of gossip with Lady Merrivale when the latter suddenly put up her lorgnette as though unable to believe the evidence of her own eyes. 'Whoever is that dancing with Max? Surely it cannot be . . .' She rapped Mrs Osmond imperatively on the arm. 'What is this, ma'am? You did not tell me that Alys had taken to dancing!'

'Alys? Where? No, no . . . I am sure you must be mistaken!' Mrs Osmond peered in the direction indicated by her companion. 'Oh, the dear child!' Her eyes misted over. 'What a sly puss . . . Max, too, to keep it from me! Ah, but doesn't she look well? '

Indeed, Alys was acquitting herself with such grace and fluency that, unbeknown to her, the other couples had moved to the side of the floor to allow Max the freedom to enable her to express herself to the full. When the music came to an end, they all applauded warmly, and the sound mingled with the triumphant pealing of bells from every church tower in Vienna.

'I wanted it to be a complete surprise,' she confessed when, breathless and pink from her exertions, she had to endure the playful scolding of Cousin Carrie. 'Oh, but I was so nervous!'

It was in this happy mood, with Sophia relaxed and enjoying herself in the best possible way with no shortage of partners, that Lottie presently found herself alone with Max. They had grown much closer of late. He was a very easy person to be with – quietly humorous, intelligent, considerate – all the qualities that she most admired in a man. Sophia had even begun to give her little sidelong looks whenever Max was mentioned.

It still came as a surprise, however, when, soon after Alys' triumph, and with everyone in the gayest of moods, Max gradually grew silent – even a little edgy, which was unusual for him. In the middle of their dance he suddenly swept her out of the room and into a small salon off the hall where, quite abruptly, he proposed.

'I had meant to wait,' he said wryly. 'But I think I have been a little in love with you from that very first moment when I saw you looking down at me from the balcony with such an endearing air of guilt – like a child caught out in a misdemeanour! Even then I thought you beautiful!'

'Oh Max!' In spite of her confusion, of the sheer gravity of such a moment, her mouth curved in memory. 'I was so mortified – and it wasn't even my handkerchief – it was Sophia's!'

This brought a faint answering smile as he took her hand in his. 'It wasn't the handkerchief I fell in love with – though I didn't recognize it as love at the time.' He waited for a reply, then said, with an abruptness that hid his shyness, 'Am I to have an answer?'

Lottie wished he hadn't asked her. *You need a husband*, Alexei had said, and perhaps he was right. Max would make a wonderful husband, loving and kind – so why did she hesitate? She was fond of him, perhaps she even loved him, and a part of her wanted to say 'yes' to him at once. Only where was the exhilaration? She felt unaccountably flat. And then she saw his face, carefully schooled in preparation for her refusal.

She held out her hands to him impulsively. 'Oh, my dear – how dreadfully ungrateful I must appear! I am deeply honoured, but if I might just have a little time to think? There are so many considerations – Sophia – my duty to her father . . .' She caught his eye and laughed a little breathlessly. 'Does that sound *very* unromantic? I don't mean it to be – '

'Don't go on!' Max said, drawing her close. 'Take all the time you need, just so long as you say "yes" at the end of it!'

His kiss was full of a quiet persuasive passion – and promised more, and it was not his fault that just for an instant Lottie found one corner of her mind making comparisons. As if to compensate for this unwitting act of betrayal, she returned his kiss with so much ardour that he was encouraged to pursue his cause more thoroughly.

They returned to the ballroom at last to find that Prince Paul had arrived – in search of his niece, he said, to give her his New Year greetings. He had come alone, and Lottie feared, from the disturbing glitter in his eyes, that he might have been seeing the New Year in rather too well.

Paul wasn't sure why he had come; at least he wasn't sure until he saw Lottie come into the ballroom from the deuce knew where, her colour heightened, and Annesley with that smug look on his face that made him want to plant his fist right in the middle of it! A dangerous unpredictable smile curled his mouth. *That* would bring the New Year in with a bang!

'Your Highness?'

A soft diffident voice at his side made him swing round. Alys Annesley was there, her face lifted towards him in that curious listening way she had, and looking full of a kind of suppressed radiance that threatened to burst out at any moment. 'I have just danced my first waltz in public,' she said with shy eagerness. 'And it is all thanks to you!'

The sarcastic retort that had been on his lips died without utterance, faced with her gentle innocence. His face softened. 'Then don't you think I am owed at least one dance by way of recompense?' And he threw Lottie a look that dared her or her tame beau to deny it to him.

Much later, going home in the coach through the festive crowds of people thronging the Graben and other main thoroughfares, Alys still seemed unusually elated, and Mrs Osmond very much feared the excitement might all have been too much for her.

'To have danced not just with your brother, but with a *prince*, my love! It is quite an accolade, is it not?'

'Humgudgeon!' Max uttered crossly. 'The fellow has the cheek of the devil!'

Lottie could not have agreed more, but she felt obliged to say dryly, 'So he may have, my dear Max, but pray remember that he also happens to be Sophia's uncle!'

Sophia's laugh spilled out. 'Oh, I don't mind! Uncle Paul is a little like the devil sometimes!'

Lottie had not been many minutes in her room when Josef came to say that Mr Annesley was very sorry to disturb her, but he must see her on a matter of some urgency. She hurried out to find him pacing the floor.

'Lottie – have you seen Alys?'

She stared at him, not comprehending. 'But she is in her room, surely?'

'No, that's just it – she isn't! She isn't anywhere,' he said looking haggard. 'And Carrie is in hysterics – '

'I'll come right away,' she said.'Josef, don't wait up. You can leave the door ajar.'

'If there is any way I can be of help, Baroness?' said the old man, ignoring her instructions. As if he could be expected to retire at such a moment!

'Oh, well . . .' She smiled at him. 'I don't suppose there will be, but if you wish to wait.'

She and Max were halfway across the landing when she heard a slight sound. The door to the ballroom was off the latch and a faint chink of light caught her eye. 'One moment,' she said, and moved across to push the door wider, with Max one step behind her.

A single branch of candles cast an almost ghostly glow over the room; the faces of the many mirrors shone blackly against the paler background, picking up in each as they passed, the slowly circling figures who were so wrapped up in each other that they were quite unaware that they were discovered. Ferdie was humming quietly beneath his breath and Alys' head was resting confidently against his shoulder.

10

Lottie awoke early with a vague feeling of foreboding, and almost at once remembered the events of a few hours ago. It had been quite dreadful – the moment the young couple had realized they were discovered, the look of frozen despair on Alys' face as Ferdie's attempts to explain were cut short. Max had not shouted. In fact he had shown remarkably little emotion – Lottie would have been less worried if he had. He simply refused to discuss anything before morning.

While she was toying with a lonely breakfast – the Fräulein took hers separately, and Sophia was still fast asleep – Josef brought her a note that had been pushed under the door. It was from Ferdie Graber.

Gnädige Baroness,

My deepest apologies for any trouble and embarrassment you may suffer as a result of my thoughtlessness. Believe me when I say that my feelings for Alys are of the very deepest, and that they are returned in full measure. My error was in supposing that what I dreamed of could ever be possible. A struggling musician with few prospects has no business to encourage one who is the sweetest and dearest soul on this earth, even to hope that we could make a life together, though were she mine, I would cherish her above all things. In light of all this, *Gnädige* Baroness, I must regretfully discontinue my lessons with Her Royal Highness. It will be better, I think, if I go away for a while. My thanks for all your kindness to me . . .

Lottie reread the letter twice, swallowing a lump in her throat. Then she pushed her cup aside and hurried in search of Josef.

'When did this come, do you know?' she asked him.

He shrugged. 'Who is to say, Baroness? An hour since, maybe two . . .'

But he was talking to the air. Lottie was running out to the landing and up the stairs, right up to the attic. She hammered on the door until Eugene's muffled voice from the adjoining room begged the gods to strike down whoever was making such a din. But at last the door opened and Ferdie stood there, still in his clothes of the night before, minus his glasses, blue-jawed and looking as though he had not closed his eyes.

'Can I come in?' she said crisply.

He frowned, mumbled something about the place being like a sty and then, when he saw she would not be discouraged, he shrugged and stood aside.

'Are you alone?'

'Yes. Lorenz has gone out to give a lesson.'

'Good.' She moved aside a pile of manuscripts, and sat in the only chair remotely habitable. It crossed her mind briefly that perhaps he was right – Alys could never hope to survive in such cluttered surroundings. And then she remembered the way they had looked in those brief moments before their world had fallen in on them.

'Have you got some good strong coffee?' she said. 'Because we have a lot of serious talking to do.'

It was about an hour later when she entered the Annesley apartment. There was no sign of the ladies, but Max was in the dining room, staring into the fire and, from the untouched state of the table, had enjoyed his breakfast as little as anyone else in the house that morning.

'Lottie!' He looked up as she came in and, though he was shaved and immaculately dressed as always, the look of distress in his eyes was not dissimilar to that she had seen in Ferdie Graber's.

He hurried across the room and took her outstretched hands. 'Thank God you are come! For almost the first time in my life, I am completely at a loss! And Cousin Carrie is prostrate with a migraine!'

Lottie felt for him, but decided that nothing would be gained by succumbing to gloom. 'Then it's just as well that I *have* come.'

Her brisk cheerfulness was a little hard to take in the circumstances. He couldn't help noticing how trim and fresh she was looking in spite of all that had happened, and wondered that she could appear so unmoved. It made his own manner rather more reserved as he led her to a chair. She smiled up at him, not without sympathy.

'My dear, do stop looking at me like that, and let us try to be practical. It isn't the end of the world, you know.'

'Nor is it a matter to be taken lightly,' he said, with more than a hint of reproof in his voice. 'If Alys were your sister you might take a different view.'

'I might, but I don't think I would. How *is* Alys this morning?'

'I have no idea,' he said harshly. 'She has not as yet found the courage to face me, though I doubt she is sleeping!'

Lottie knew that it was only the shock and the worry that made him speak of Alys like that. She was his beloved sister, on whom he had lavished all his care – and now he felt betrayed.

'You don't think perhaps she is too distressed to come out?' He did not answer, though his mouth tightened a little, like a man in pain. 'Well, never mind, I think we might be better off without her for the moment. Max, what do you mean to do about Alys and Ferdie?'

'Do?' He sounded suddenly anguished. 'What can I do? This is exactly my dilemma. God knows, whatever I do she is going to be hurt. If only I had seen this coming!'

'Well, you should have. It has been obvious any time these past few weeks.'

Max stared. 'You knew?'

'I guessed,' she said, looking back at him without the least hint of embarrassment.

'And you didn't think to tell me?'

'My dear Max, there was very little to tell. It was all so very innocent. Besides,' she said, head high, 'I am not in the habit of tale-bearing!'

'Oh, good God!' He sprang to his feet, running agitated fingers through his carefully brushed hair. 'Lottie, can't you see how impossible the whole thing is? A penniless musician!'

'A very gifted musician,' she insisted. 'Did you know that Ferdie's compositions have been praised most highly by Beethoven himself? With a suitable sponsor, who can say how far he may not go?'

'That doesn't alter the fact that Alys is . . . is not like everyone else.'

'So,' Lottie suggested quietly, 'are you saying that she is to be denied love and happiness because she is blind? That she must spend the rest of her life in your care?'

'No!' Max was beginning to look harassed. 'That's the last thing I want for her! But even you must admit that her needs are very special? How can she possibly hope to fend for herself in a strange country and in God knows what state of penury?'

Lottie took Ferdie's letter from her pocket and gave it to him. He read it in silence, folded it and gave it back to her.

'Hm.' He was clearly fighting a battle with his conscience. 'The fellow obviously cares for her, but perhaps it might be for the best if he goes away,' he said slowly.

'No!'

Alys had come into the room, unnoticed by them. She looked very pale and agitated, but not tearful.

'My dear!' Max went quickly to her side, and brought her forward to her chair by the fire. But she was unwilling to sit.

'Max, I must see Ferdie! He mustn't be allowed to go away! What happened wasn't his fault. I had to persuade him to meet me in the ballroom. We wanted to begin the New Year together. We . . .' Her voice faltered and then firmed. 'We want to be married. *Please* don't be against us!'

'I'm not, oh my dearest girl, I'm not!' Max took her in his arms and Lottie felt a prick behind her eyes. 'If you really love your musician then I would be the last to stand in your way! But I think I had better see this young man before we go any further.' He dropped a kiss on her forehead. 'I shall need a great many assurances before I entrust my sister to anyone's care!'

Lottie stood up, satisfied that all would now go well. 'Then I can safely leave you to arrange matters. Shall I tell Ferdie you'll see him? I expect he is pacing the floor outside. Poor man, he looked so very distrait when I saw him earlier!'

'You have seen Ferdie this morning?' Alys turned a shining face towards her, her hands held out. 'Oh Lottie – how good you are! Is he dreadfully miserable?'

'I hope not any more. We did a lot of straight talking and came to some amicable conclusions. Now he should simply be nervous, as any young man in his position would be!'

'Conclusions?' Max was eyeing her quizzically.

'Well, somebody had to do something quickly.' A note of

defiance entered her voice. 'So I have decided to become his sponsor.'

'I see,' Max said dryly.

'Oh Lottie!' whispered Alys.

Lottie kissed her. As Max walked with her to the door she was very much aware that he was still looking at her.

'I assume you can afford to sponsor young Graber?' he asked with deceptive mildness.

'Of course. And I mean to ask Prince Adolphus to help him also.'

To her surprise he began to laugh. 'Lottie Raimund – what can I say? Do you always get your way?'

She wrinkled her nose at him. 'Not always. But if something is wrong and one can see a way to right it, one should at least make a push to do so, don't you think?'

He kissed her with sudden ardour. 'I think I would be a lucky man to win you,' he said, and let her go.

In the hall Ferdie Graber waited, pacing nervously and pulling at his cravat. Lottie watched the two men shake hands and left them to come to terms.

Sophia thought the whole affair vastly romantic, and was only sorry that she had missed most of the drama. This led Lottie to hope devoutly that she would not in turn fancy herself in love with Eugene who came almost daily to work on her portrait. But Fräulein Lanner was obviously filled with similar forebodings and never left them alone for a moment, casting a distinct gloom over the proceedings.

In spite of this, however, the portrait was coming along beautifully, and Lottie had no regrets for she was sure that Prince Adoplphus would be pleased with the result.

Meanwhile her own life continued very busy. The weather turned very cold and one afternoon when returning from a visit to friends, Mrs Osmond slipped on the icy cobblestones as she stepped from the carriage and sprained her knee.

'How could I have been so careless?' she reiterated tearfully and for the umpteenth time to Lottie when she visited her. 'And just when Alys most needs me! We have been going out almost daily, you know, to see what may be found for her by way of a suitable house or ground-floor apartment, though this is hardly an auspicious moment with everywhere so overcrowded!'

Poor Mrs Osmond! She had not yet come to terms with Alys' impending marriage. To calm her, Lottie offered her own services.

'Though I'm sure that Max and Ferdie between them are perfectly capable of knowing what is needed.'

'Oh, men!' the other exclaimed. 'What can they possibly know of a woman's needs? Why they cannot live in England when they are married I'm sure I don't know!'

It was useless to explain to her that Ferdie's work and inspiration lay in Vienna. So Lottie found herself going out regularly with Max and Alys, and Ferdie if he was not working, to view possible properties. And wherever they went, the mongrel dog trotted faithfully behind the coach.

'Ferdie has christened him Fidelio,' said Alys, much moved by the dog's devotion to her. 'After that marvellously faithful character in Beethoven's opera, you know.'

Such expeditions were not very exciting for Sophia, however, and were usually undertaken when she was either studying or was invited elsewhere with friends, as happened more often now.

On one such day, when Sophia was confined to the apartment with a cold, Lottie returned to find her in a state of near hysteria. She could get little sense from her except for some garbled nonsense about Countess von Deiter, so she questioned Josef. From him she learned that the Countess had indeed called, and then he hesitated.

'Come on, Josef. You are at liberty to say exactly what you wish.'

'Well, Baroness, I don't know what was said,' he admitted, 'but voices were raised, and after the Countess left, it got worse rather than better.'

They exchanged a look that said everything. 'Thank you, Josef,' she said, and went in search of Fräulein Lanner.

'Her Royal Highness is behaving very foolishly, Baroness,' said the governess coldly. 'One can only assume that it arises from her present feverishness.'

Lottie could hardly contain her anger. 'We will leave your opinions aside, if you please, Fräulein. I want to know exactly what happened here this morning.'

Fräulein Lanner's manner could best be described as truculent. 'The Countess called to see you, Baroness, concerning the very important question of Her Royal Highness' future. She has been much concerned of late about the kind of company Princess Sophia has been keeping, the light-minded influences to which she has been subjected – '

'Of which you, no doubt, have kept her well informed,' Lottie said icily. 'But go on.'

'Finding the Princess alone –' her tone implied neglect on Lottie's part '– Countess von Deiter took it upon herself to remind the child of her duty – a quality which I have done my best to instil, but which you, Baroness, have undermined at every stage!'

Bitterness and frustration were making Fräulein Lanner careless.

'She came to tell you – and Her Royal Highness – that Duke von Gratz has written to Prince Adolphus to offer for her hand, and that it is her duty to accept what can only be regarded as a most excellent match.'

Lottie could by now hardly bring herself to speak, but she had to know. 'And has the Duke received an answer from Prince Adolphus?'

'I believe not, as yet.' The Fräulein almost smirked. 'But he can hardly be so short-sighted as to reject what must be an ideal suitor.'

Lottie went once more in search of Sophia and found her face down upon her bed, red-eyed and utterly wretched.

'Darling girl.' Lottie stroked back her dark, damp curls. 'You really mustn't upset yourself so, or you will make yourself ill.'

'But if I have to marry Duke Franz . . .'

'You won't,' Lottie said firmly. 'I promise you that whatever happens, I won't let you marry that man!'

Sophia sat up a little. 'But if Papa orders it . . .'

'He won't,' Lottie said, and prayed that she was right.

Sophia drew a shuddering breath. 'Fräulein told me . . . things, about b-babies and being married. She said that I would have t-to submit, that it would be my duty . . . Oh, but Baroness Lottie, if I had to permit Duke Franz to do such things to me, I think I would sooner die!'

That awful warped woman, Lottie raged silently, as she tried to convince Sophia that the governess had explained matters very clumsily, and that the expression of love between a man and a woman could and should be a pleasurable experience.

'Was it so for you, Baroness?' the Princess asked suddenly, intense curiosity in her tear-drenched eyes.

Lottie's glance slid away as she said lightly, but with scrupulous truth, 'My husband treated me always with gentleness and consideration, and I'm sure that when you are married, the same will be true for you.'

This equivocal answer appeared to satisfy Sophia, and Lottie could only pray that the crude ravings of that unlovely, unfulfilled bitch would have no lasting effect upon the young impressionable girl, and that her father would soon set all their minds at ease.

When at last Sophia was calm enough to be left, Lottie went in search of Fräulein Lanner once more. Without any polite preliminaries she ordered the governess to pack her bags and go – at once. The Fräulein tried to bluster her way out.

'You have no right to do this! I am not employed by you. Only His Serene Highness can dismiss me!'

'Then you may return to Gellenstadt and make your protests to His Serene Highness,' Lottie said implacably. 'I shall most certainly be writing to him to explain my actions in full! For the moment, my duty is to Sophia, and I tell you that you will not remain another night under this roof, nor have any further contact with her. I have given instructions to that effect.'

The Fräulein departed, still protesting. When she had gone, Lottie scrawled an angry note to Prince Paul, demanding a meeting with him somewhere away from the apartment. Then she set out to confront the Countess von Deiter.

11

A reply had come from Prince Paul. It was awaiting her when she returned, emotionally shattered, from her confrontation with Countess von Deiter. His note was brief, almost curt – informing her that he would arrive to collect her at four o'clock. It did little to lift her spirits.

But there was no time to brood. With the angry words of her quarrel with Countess von Deiter still churning round in her brain, she was forced to put on a welcoming smile as callers began to arrive. Several young men, hopeful of seeing Sophia, were hard put to it to hide their disappointment upon being informed that she was indisposed, though most were gallant enough to stay and talk to her for considerably longer than politeness demanded.

Lady Merrivale called in, having visited Mrs Osmond – and in spite of her own worries, Lottie noticed at once that her ladyship was not her usual self.

'Is something wrong?' she asked, drawing Lady Merrivale to one side.

'Oh, my dear, the very worst has happened! My poor Arabella!' The statuesque figure seemed somehow to have shrunk a little.

'Ma'am, you alarm me!' Lottie exclaimed. 'Has Arabella come to some kind of harm?'

'The very worst kind, and if it is not all round Vienna within the day, I shall be very much surprised!' Lady Merrivale dabbed furtively at her eyes and announced in tragic tones, 'Count Laurien has run off with Lady Sarah, and my poor child is heartbroken!'

Lottie just stopped herself saying, 'Oh, is that all?' and instead made suitable noises of commiseration.

'I always said that woman was treacherous! Of course, it was his money she was after, but she will be well served, for I am sure he has no thought of marrying her!'

'Quite,' said Lottie, knowing full well that Lady Sarah was

an exceedingly wealthy woman in her own right, and knew exactly what she was doing.

'We shall go home immediately, of course. Arabella vows she cannot face *anyone*, and I'm sure I don't blame her.'

Again Lottie said all that was proper, and though she would have liked to be very much less charitable about her precious Arabella, a certain fondness for Lady Merrivale made any such observation impossible. How would Max take the news, she wondered.

Her visitors had all left by three o'clock, leaving her ample time to dress and, with Sophia now fast asleep, to assemble her thoughts so that Prince Paul should not have her at a disadvantage.

Her anger had abated somewhat in the course of being pleasant to people, and to sharpen it she went over in her mind all that had happened – Sophia's distress, the Fräulein's inhuman treatment of the child, and the utter effrontery of the Countess' behaviour when confronted.

'I can spare you five minutes,' had been her greeting when Lottie was announced. 'My husband and I have been invited to attend upon Monsieur de Talleyrand at the Kaunitz Palace. His niece, Madame Eduard de Périgord, said that he had asked most particularly to see the Count,' she concluded pompously.

'Then you may be sure he wants something.' Lottie pricked the bubble of her conceit and watched the Countess' mouth tighten in anger. 'However, what I have to say won't take five minutes. It is simply this – don't you ever *dare* to come into my home again in my absence and presume to read Her Royal Highness a lecture as to her duties and obligations. As a result of your meddling and that of Fräulein Lanner, the Princess is now in a severe state of shock.'

The Countess' face was turning an unbecoming shade of purple which went ill with her brassy hair. She began to expostulate about Lottie's own ill manners, but was cut short.

'I have dismissed Fräulein Lanner, and she is already gone, so she can no longer come tale-bearing to you.' A tiny gasp showed that this thrust had hit the mark. 'I wish I could do the same with you, but I cannot. However, if you so much as attempt to approach Sophia in the immediate future, I will not be responsible for my actions!'

She had left upon that note, with screaming imprecations ringing in her ears, and shaking with the force of her emotions.

This recollection so moved her that she was more than ready for Prince Paul, who arrived promptly, driving his own four-in-hand. He was wearing a heavy flowing coat with several capes, the topmost one fashioned of sable. He eyed her own ivory redingote dourly. It was fastened high at the neck and trimmed with fur, and the close fitting bonnet was also trimmed with fur.

'Will you be warm enough?' he said abruptly, as he handed her up into the curricle.

'That depends upon how far you intend to travel,' she replied, equalling his manner.

'Not far.' The vehicle swayed on its springs as he leaped up beside her, reached for a thick woollen rug which he tucked around her with meticulous thoroughness, and dismissed his groom who was holding the horses' heads. They sprang forward and she felt the immediate rush of cold air that made her glad of the rug.

'Where *are* we going?' she asked at last when they had cleared the town and were on the road to Schönbrunn.

'A hunting lodge belonging to a friend of mine,' he said without taking his eyes off the road. The horses were fresh and, with a thin layer of snow down, more skill than usual was needed. 'I gathered that you wished for somewhere where we could be private. I ought to have felt flattered,' he added with deep irony.

She pushed her fur collar up round her face to mask it from his view and declined to be drawn. It seemed no time at all before they were turning in at the gates of a small estate and following a winding drive until a small turreted house came into view.

'Oh, how pretty it is!' she exclaimed, surprised out of her self-imposed silence.

An obsequious manservant showed them into a delightfully comfortable-looking room where a cheerful fire leaped and crackled in the sudden draught.

'Will you take some refreshment now or later, sir?' murmured the manservant.

Prince Paul quirked an eyebrow at Lottie, who shook her head. 'No refreshments, Hugo.'

The manservant bowed and withdrew, closing the doors silently as he went.

'He thinks we are here for a little amatory dalliance,' Paul said, stripping off his gauntlets and flinging them down on a bureau top. He opened his coat, and held out his hands to the fire, turning his head briefly to look up at Lottie. 'I feel sure he is wrong. Why are we here?'

Lottie too had loosened the fastenings at her neck. She said evenly, 'You don't know?'

'I assume you wish to quarrel with me. Other than that . . .' He shrugged.

'I want all this nonsense with your friend von Gratz stopped,' she said.

'Nonsense?' He straightened up and faced her.

'You will presumably be aware that he has written to your brother to offer for Sophia? I don't know how far you encouraged him, but I can make a fairly shrewd guess.'

'Based on what evidence? Have you been paying Baron Hager's agents to spy on me?' he said cuttingly. 'The Emperor's secret police chief deals in trivialities, I believe. He has paid agents everywhere – rummaging in peoples' wastepaper baskets looking for anything suspicious.'

'I don't need secret police,' Lottie exclaimed, annoyed at being put in the wrong. 'I need only to use my eyes to see the way you and Duke Franz and the von Deiters are for ever in corners – and all too often a Bavarian representative is there with you, too.'

He came towards her, his eyes slate-hard and calculating. 'You have an overfertile imagination, lovely Lottie. It could get you into serious trouble one day.'

She stood her ground and he stopped just short of her. 'There is nothing in the least sinister in a group of people talking.' His mouth smiled, but his eyes did not. 'Whatever do you suppose we are plotting?'

'To sell out Gellenstadt to Bavaria,' she said quietly. 'Through von Gratz. Prince Adolphus is slowly dying.' She found the words hard to say, but they had to be said. 'We all know it – and once your friend is married to Sophia, you will be able to manipulate things between you exactly as you please.' She hesitated. 'Duke Franz seemed to be under the impression that I, too, might be ripe for manipulation – if you take my meaning? Or perhaps you arranged that between you, also?'

Paul's face darkened. Without warning his hands closed round her neck, not tightly but with just sufficient pressure, his thumbs caressing her throat gently as she fought down fear. He said with menacing softness, 'You really are talking the most arrant nonsense, you know.'

'Am I?'

She forced the words out, holding his eyes with hers.

'What exactly did Franz say?'

'Nothing very specific, but the message was unmistakable.'

After a moment, he frowned and released her, pushing her away almost violently. 'Crazy girl,' he said angrily. 'You have lived too long in my brother's shadow and are become afflicted with his suspicions. But don't make his mistake in thinking that I don't care about Gellenstadt – I do, quite as much as he does, if not more!'

'You don't show it!' Lottie fingered her neck absently.

'When have I ever been encouraged to show it? Any opinion that doesn't accord with my brother's is immediately suspect. He is so entrenched in his own view of Gellenstadt that he can't see it's so turned in upon itself that if there aren't some radical changes soon it will dwindle into a tired old age, because most of the men under thirty will have left to seek greater challenges elsewhere.' He was striding about the room now, restless, flushed, his voice bitter. 'But if I presume to express that opinion, I am damned as a rebellious troublemaker.'

He turned to glare at her. 'In point of fact, it's so long since Adolphus has set foot beyond his boundaries that he's forgotten there's another world out here!'

Lottie had never seen Paul so impassioned, and in spite of her loyalties to Prince Adolphus she was moved by his argument.

'But don't you see that if Duke von Gratz gets his hands on the country it will get swallowed up by Bavaria and he'll bleed the silver mines dry in no time for his own gain – and we shall still go under!'

Prince Paul stopped his pacing. 'Do you really believe I would let that happen?'

'I think . . . Oh, I don't know what I believe any more!'

He came back to her and, taking her by the shoulders, shook her slightly. 'Oh, Lottie, Lottie!'

His touch and the tone of his voice threatened her composure, but she must not be put off. 'Except,' she said firmly, 'that I know von Gratz must not be allowed to marry Sophia.'

She told him as graphically as she could what had occurred earlier, and how distressed Sophia was as a result. Paul's mouth tightened.

'A pity,' he said, 'but she'll get over it. Young girls must learn the facts of life sooner or later.' His fingers dug into the tops of her arms. 'They can't all live in little ivory towers!'

'Oh!' she gasped, her throat tight.

'Well, I'm sorry, my dear, but it could be said that you are not a fit person to pass an opinion on such matters,' he said harshly. 'Sophia has a rôle to fulfil. It is better that she should learn early *all* that will be required of her.'

'But not like that!' she cried angrily. 'Not from a perverted, dried-up harridan like Fräulein Lanner! It will be wonderful if she has not given Sophia a lasting revulsion of men! And it might never have happened but for Countess von Deiter's meddling. Was it your idea to send her?'

Paul shook her quite hard. 'No, devil take it, it was not! You seem determined to set the blame for everything at my door! Whatever kind of man do you take me for?'

Lottie said nothing, but looked pointedly at his fingers still painfully digging into her arms. Abruptly he let her go and flung away from her.

'All right, I admit that Franz has grown more ruthless and ambitious with the years, but that doesn't mean I can't handle him *and* the von Deiters. As for Sophia,' he said over his shoulder, 'she will be safe enough. Adolphus hates Franz almost as much as you do, so he's hardly likely to favour the match. If I'm wrong, then I shall take it upon myself to discourage him – but in my own way.' Paul swung back to glare at her. 'Now will you be satisfied?'

And reluctantly she was obliged to admit that there was little more to be done.

Sophia did in fact recover quite quickly, but Lottie suspected that the improvement was only superficial as she became noticeably less easy in her manner towards Count Enghein and her other would-be beaux than before. Strangely enough, she was most at ease with Alexei, in whom Lottie had confided, and who for all his flirtatious ways managed to handle her with an expert blend of teasing and friendliness that posed no threat.

The fact that Fräulein Lanner was no longer around seemed to help also, and Lottie devoted all her energies to keeping the young girl entertained so that she would have no time to brood. The best tonic of all, however, came in a letter from Prince Adolphus confirming that he would not entertain the idea of von Gratz as a son-in-law.

There was no mention in his letter of Fräulein Lanner, so Lottie could only assume that he had not yet received any word from her or the von Deiters. He did however urge Lottie to fresh efforts with regard to settling Sophia's future and, in spite of the drawback of age, showed some interest in Count Enghein as a possible candidate.

A sleighing party projected by the Austrian court also proved to be an excellent diversion. A great number of sleighs had been refurbished and all now waited upon the weather.

'They are quite beautiful!' Sophia told Alys excitedly after Prince Paul had taken her to see the royal sleighs. 'Those intended for the sovereigns are in the form of a *calèche*. They have emerald velvet cushions trimmed with gold and are all gaily coloured with lots of gold paint everywhere! And the other sleighs are almost as beautiful! All the harnesses will have silver bells . . . Oh, I do wish it would *snow*!'

'My niece seems to have made a remarkable recovery,' Prince Paul remarked with some irony to Lottie as he listened. He had, to give him his due, gone out of his way to indulge Sophia in the days that had followed Lottie's attack upon him, and the young girl hardly noticed that he and the Baroness scarcely spoke to one another.

'Don't be fooled,' Lottie said. 'Sophia's apparent gaiety is still a fairly fragile thing.'

'Well, no doubt she will be relieved to know that Franz is no longer a threat,' he observed dryly. 'He, on the other hand, is furious. I have seldom seen him in such an ugly mood, and I fear he lays the blame squarely at your door, my dear.'

'I believe I can bear his displeasure more easily than his attempts to please,' she retorted.

'Well, I advise you to have a care, for all that,' he said grimly.

At last it snowed, and the snow was followed by a severe frost which provided the ideal surface for the sleighs to proceed. The imperial promenade was agreed upon and the final preparations made. From early morning on the day appointed, huge crowds gathered on the Josef Platz to cheer the party on its way. The cold clear air rang with the tinkling of bells as the many spirited blood horses, richly caparisoned with tiger skins and rich furs, their flowing manes plaited with knots and ribbons of many hues, stamped the ground in their eagerness to be off. Not until two o'clock did the sovereigns come down to take their places, but the sight was worth waiting for. Each cavalier had a lady, the procession being led by the Emperor of Austria with Elizabeth of Russia, the latter wrapped in a coat of green velvet lined with ermine, and set in her toque of the same colour, an aigrette of diamonds. The ladies who followed were equally richly adorned. To escort the six royal sleighs came twenty-four young pages in medieval costumes, and a squadron of the Hungarian Nobiliary Guards – and all preceded by a detachment of cavalry, the sergeants' caterers of the Court on horseback, and an immense sleigh drawn by six horses, containing an orchestra of kettledrums and trumpets – and immediately preceding the Emperor, his grand equerry, Trautmansdorf and his men at arms.

Thirty other sledges followed the royal ones, and the throats of the watching throngs had grown hoarse from cheering by the time the last one had traversed the Vienna streets in slow and stately procession. Then, at a given signal, the horses set off at a gallop for Schönbrunn. The whole day was a magical experience for Sophia who was wrapped to the ears in ermine, and displayed pink cheeks and sparkling eyes to bewitch Count Enghein and many others besides. Franz von Gratz had elected to stay away, so there was nothing to mar the occasion for her.

For Lottie it was not simply magical – it was also to be

memorable in a quite unexpected way. Picnicking in a white wonderland with music and the crackle of great bonfires gave one a feeling of total unreality, she found, and with Max at her side, mingling with the other guests, she was happier than she had been for some time; even the presence of Prince Paul with his latest inamorata had not the power to diminish her contentment.

The Czar had been marginally less persistent of late, though this had been in some part due to his being laid up with a slight indisposition. But now he was in much better spirits – the Polish question was on the point of being settled in his favour, and the sight of Lottie in blue velvet lavishly trimmed with sable and wearing a dashing close-fitting sable toque trimmed with curling ostrich feathers, dyed to the same blue and secured with a pin of sapphires and diamonds, fired him with renewed desire.

He tried several times to persuade Lottie to walk with him, away from the rest, not deterred even by the presence of his Empress, until Lottie was almost at her wit's end to know how to fend him off without giving offence or drawing undue attention to her efforts.

'My dear Lottie. I have been looking everywhere for you!'

It was Max, hurrying across to her, his face wearing that rather reserved expression that could be so misleading. In a relief that was born of desperation she extended a hand to him, and turned an arch smile upon Alexander.

'Oh, la, sire, here is my fiancé come to catch us together! And how fierce he looks, to be sure!' She lowered her voice. 'In truth, he is inclined to be jealous, though I am sure he must be aware that in Your Majesty's case, there can be no possible cause for anything of the kind!'

The Czar looked slightly put out, Max was frowning at her in disbelief which might well be construed as annoyance – and lifting her eyes slightly, Lottie saw Prince Paul standing not more than a few feet away.

He could not but help overhearing what she said, and though their glances locked for no more than seconds, Lottie felt her heart squeezing in her breast until she could hardly breathe, for looking into his eyes was a little like looking into a very personal and private hell.

12

'Did you really mean it?' Max said when the Czar had somewhat churlishly given them leave to depart his presence.

Lottie, still reeling from Prince Paul's unexpectedly violent reaction to her revelation, was slow to answer. Then she became aware that Max was looking at her anxiously and she made a desperate effort to pull herself together, putting as much feeling into her voice as she could muster.

'My dear, of course I meant it!' she exclaimed. 'I had not intended to tell you so in quite such a dramatic way, of course – but it just slipped out! You aren't cross with me, are you?'

He took her hand. 'Come behind this tree and I'll show you exactly how I feel!'

This *is* what I want, she told herself as he kissed her, and she gave herself up to it without reserve. And then somehow the word had run around like wildfire and they were being congratulated on all sides, so that by the time they travelled home in the moonlight, through a glittering white landscape that seemed totally unreal, with the lanterns bobbing and bells jingling, and everyone in the greatest good humour, she had almost forgotten that one jarring moment when she had come face to face with Paul.

He was with his voluptuous brunette and, by the glitter of his eyes, had been drinking. He had stared down at her for a moment in silence. Then, with a very faint slur in his voice he had said softly: 'Lottie Raimund – you are a fool!'

There were other repercussions, of course. Some pleasant, some less so. Alys was overjoyed.

'I could not be happier, dearest Lottie! You have been so good to me, and now I am to have you for a sister. It is almost more than I can take in. Perhaps we might even have a double wedding!'

But this was too much for Lottie to contemplate. 'There are so many things that I must do before I can even begin to decide on a date,' she said hastily.

Alys was silent, a small frown creasing her brow. 'But . . . if you are in love with Max, could you not marry him and then do these things? I know that I want to marry Ferdie just as soon as it can be arranged!'

Lottie bit her lip. She would have to be careful in her discussions with Alys. She could pick up a false note in the voice where no one else would spot it.

'Yes, I know, my dear,' she said with perfect truth. 'But I do have responsibilities . . . Prince Adolphus is counting on me to look after Sophia, and it really wouldn't be fair to him – to Sophia, or even to Max, if I were so selfish as to put my own happiness first.'

'No, of course not! I do see that.' Alys was immediately contrite. 'It's just that I am so happy myself that I want everyone else to be happy, too.'

'But I *am* happy,' Lottie said, and convinced herself that she meant it.

Sophia, however, had been a little quiet since the day of the sleighing party, and although she had been as warm in her congratulations as everyone else, Lottie had a feeling that her engagement to Max was at the back of it. And when Lottie finally tackled her, it all came tumbling out.

'I shan't know how to go on without you! Oh, Baroness Lottie, what am I going to do if I have to return to Gellenstadt alone? There will be only Papa and Grandmama – no one to talk to or laugh with!'

Lottie gathered the Princess into her arms. 'My dear child, there is no question of me abandoning you! As if I could! Mr Annesley is a very understanding man . . . you must know that. He would never want you to be hurt in any way! We just need a little time to work things out, that's all.'

But it wasn't quite as simple as she made it sound. Max had obligations in England, too. His uncle, the earl, was not a young man and relied on him for many things. Already, he had stayed longer in Vienna than he had originally intended.

'It may be,' she broached the idea diffidently, 'that we shall have to part for a little while, Max. Would you mind most dreadfully?'

'Yes, of course I would mind,' he said. 'I keep having the oddest notion that if I let you out of my sight, I may lose you.'

He smiled wryly. 'But it seems to be the only way we are going to resolve matters.'

It had been rumoured for some time that Lord Castlereagh was to return to England, and finally the rumour was confirmed when he told Max one evening at dinner that he was needed back home.

'Parliament, it seems, cannot go on without me any longer,' he said dryly. 'I shall not be sorry. Perhaps a fresh mind on matters will help to resolve the awful inertia that hangs over this Congress.'

'We shall miss you and Lady Castlereagh,' Lottie said impulsively.

He smiled, that rather glacial smile. 'I believe you will be in the minority, ma'am. I do not, I fear, have sufficient light-mindedness to please most people here. Perhaps the Duke of Wellington, who is to succeed me, will do rather better.'

It seemed to Lottie that the festivities were beginning to pall a little all round. A surfeit of pleasure, like a surfeit of sweetmeats, tended to leave one feeling a trifle jaded. But Alys was so radiantly happy that she redressed the balance for them all. A small house had been found, further out of the centre of Vienna than Ferdie had hoped for, but it was so exactly what they were looking for that plans were immediately put in hand to purchase it.

Alys wanted Sophia to see it immediately, but the Princess already had an invitation to take tea with Count Enghein's sister that afternoon.

'I am so nervous,' she said. 'Baroness Lottie was to accompany me, but she has a severe headache and with a big reception this evening, she decided to rest. It is so unlike her to be even the slightest bit ill! Alys, I don't know what to do. I can't possibly go to Princess Vichenska's alone! Unless –' Sophia looked up hopefully. 'Are you busy this afternoon?'

'Why, no,' Alys said. 'I said I would sit with Cousin Carrie. In any case, I couldn't possibly –'

'Of course you could! I shall not be the only guest – at least I hope not! Count Enghein said it would be very informal, and a carriage is to be sent for us. Oh, do say you will come?'

Alys agreed, albeit reluctantly, and promptly, in fact a little early, the carriage arrived bearing an impressive crest on the door and fine velvet upholstery within. Sophia had half-hoped the Count might come himself to escort them, but he did not. The driver stayed on his box while a well-built young manservant in the finest livery helped them in and laid fur rugs across their knees with the most scrupulous care.

Alys smoothed the softness with sensitive fingers and smiled. 'I think your Count is a little in love with you.'

There was a moment's hesitation and an unmistakable restraint in Sophia's voice as she answered, 'I hope not. He is very jolly, and he likes me a lot, I think – but I don't want anyone to be in love with me.'

'Why not? It is very agreeable, I promise you.'

'No!' Sophia jerked the word out, and then laughed nervously. 'For you, perhaps, but not for me.'

Alys had heard that note of panic and wondered at it, but she had no wish to disturb Sophia just when she needed all her confidence, so she changed the subject.

The carriage stopped and Sophia looked out in some surprise. 'This doesn't look like Himmelpfort Gasse.' She leaned forward to take a closer look, and as she did so the door opened and a burly figure filled the opening. 'Who are you? Get away at once!'

Alys, sitting very still, smelled the fear; she heard the shrillness in Sophia's frightened voice, felt the added draught and knew that the door on her own side had been opened also.

'Now then, my pretties – don't do anything silly and you won't get hurt.'

'If it's money you want, or jewels – I must tell you we have very little.' Sophia, though terrified by the masked faces, found the Fräulein's rigorous training now came to her aid. 'Furthermore, we are expected at Princess Vichenska's house for tea and if we do not arrive, a hue and cry will be raised!'

'Talks well, don't she?'

The men laughed and the spokesman mocked her tones. 'Well, I'm afraid there isn't any *tea* where you're going, little Miss Highty-Tighty! We're just putting you out of harm's way for a bit, see? You can struggle and make it hard, or you can be good little girls and you won't get hurt.'

Alys hadn't understood a word, but somehow she knew that the men were dangerous and that the spokesman was the manservant who had helped them into the carriage. She spoke quietly and in English.

'Don't argue with them, Sophia. It will be better for now to do as they say. But if you see a chance to escape without endangering yourself, go. They won't harm me.'

There wasn't a soul in sight as they were bundled out of the carriage and into a mean narrow street where the upper storeys of the houses almost met above their heads.

'Hey! This one's blind!' said the other voice – and laughed.

'I know. But what can't see, can't tell tales! Eh?'

He had hardly got the words out when there was a great baying howl that would have struck terror into the bravest man, and a dark shape hurled itself through the air.

'Fidelio!' cried Alys as the man holding her suddenly let go of her with a howl of rage and fear. She stood there, uncertain how or where to move.

Sophia watched in horror as the man grappled with the enraged dog. If only her own captor would let go of her to go to his aid, she might be able to get Alys away. But it was a vain hope.

The man on the ground managed to reach into his pocket and struggled to produce a short length of wicked looking iron pipe – which he brought down with savage ferocity on Fidelio's head. The dog whined and slumped to lie inert, with blood oozing from a gaping wound.

Sophia cried out and Alys called the dog's name in a shaky voice. But the men had wasted more than enough time. They bundled the two girls through a door in the wall and down some steps lifting Alys off her feet in their urgency to get their work finished. One of them ran back to the carriage for the fur rug and flung it down after them. Then the door slammed shut and all was dark and silent except for their own sobbing breathing – and the occasional scuttering sounds that struck terror into them both.

When Sophia and Alys were late returning home, Lottie did not at first worry. After all, they were with Count Enghein and his sister, and he would be sure to escort them safely home.

The headache which had troubled her earlier still throbbed faintly, and she told herself that it was this that was responsible for vague sensations of oppression that filled her.

If only they had not to go to the Hofburg that evening – but it was to honour the Duke of Wellington, who had arrived in Vienna earlier in the week, and she could hardly not be there. She schooled herself to relax.

An hour later she was still waiting, and the oppression was fast turning to apprehension. Count Enghein and his sister were themselves attending the reception and could not possibly be keeping the girls so long.

Unable to settle a moment longer she hurried across to the Annesleys' apartment, only to find Max about to come to her.

'I thought they might be with you,' she said, trying to still the panic that threatened her.

'I'll have the horses put to at once,' Max said with a calm that she envied. 'Go there myself to see what's keeping them.' He smiled reassuringly at her, but behind his eyes she saw the same worry that gnawed at her. 'Their carriage could well have broken a trace, lost a wheel – there could be any number of explanations.'

'Yes, of course. I am being foolish, I know.' She took a deep breath and smiled back at him. 'I would come with you, but it's perhaps better that I stay . . . in case they arrive . . .'

Josef came in at that moment to say that Count Enghein had called. Lottie and Max exchanged glances. 'Show him in at once,' Lottie said.

The young man came in swiftly. He was diffident, ill at ease, but very polite.

'Forgive me, *Gnädige* Baroness. I came simply to enquire after Her Royal Highness. Her indisposition is not serious, I trust?'

At first the words did not register. When they did, her heart began to thud painfully. 'Her indisposition?' She had to force the words out.

'When we received your message, I was desolate. And as it did not stipulate the nature of the indisposition, I wondered . . . about this evening –'

Max cut in on him.

'Are you saying, Count, that Princess Sophia did not arrive at your sister's house this afternoon – that you haven't seen her?'

'But no.' His face paled as he looked from one to the other. 'I had not set out when the message arrived. Please –' His voice grew urgent. 'Please to tell me . . . what has happened?'

Lottie was trying desperately not to give way to the wild impossible thoughts that pressed in on her.

'A carriage did arrive – your sister's, we thought – at the precise time it was expected.' She closed her eyes briefly against the look on Max's face. 'And Sophia has not returned, nor Miss Annesley who accompanied her in place of myself.'

The hours that followed were by far the worst that Lottie had ever experienced. At first she was so busy that she was able to stop the worst flight of imagination from taking hold. Word travelled swiftly and soon a whole army of people were out looking for any trace of a clue that might lead to discovering the whereabouts of the two girls. Ferdie, almost out of his mind, had many contacts in the city, as had all the lodgers in the house who had grown fond of its more exalted occupants, and he and Max resolved to spend the whole night going from one to the other with dogged persistence, convinced that somewhere someone must have seen something.

Almost by the minute Lottie expected a ransom demand – it was the only logical explanation. Yet at the back of her mind she could not rid herself of a less logical one – that somehow, Franz von Gratz was at the back of it all.

Her first call had been to Am Hof. She asked for Prince Paul, and when he came, his manner was far from encouraging; she tried to ignore it, everything now being secondary to finding Sophia and Alys. She explained in a clear unemotional voice what had happened, and was treated to a clipped, penetrating inquisition that roused her to indignation in spite of her resolve.

'Well, of course I should have thought it a little odd that the Count had not come himself to escort Sophia, but I have told you I was feeling unwell!'

'Unfortunate in the circumstances, Baroness.'

Franz von Gratz had entered the room unnoticed. He sounded – she tried to define how he sounded – all smooth sympathy on the surface, but secretly rejoicing in her misery. Or was she being too fanciful?

'One has heard, of course, about the disappearance of the little Princess. I have just returned from a friend's house and the word is already on the street.' He put up his glass to watch her expression. 'And this coach with the crest upon it – it has not been identified?'

She was obliged to admit that it had not. He shrugged.

'I'll make inquiries of my own,' Prince Paul said harshly. 'Go back and wait. Should there be a demand for money, do nothing until I come.'

Lottie knew that what he said was reasonable, yet she resented his manner of saying it. And her temper was not improved when, as she was leaving, she met Countess von Deiter in the hall.

From her expression upon seeing Lottie, it was all too clear why she had come, and she lost no time in making her opinion known.

'I have always said that your care of Princess Sophia was too casual by far. And turning off Fräulein Lanner as you did was just one more blunder in a long history of mismanagement! Fortunately, the poor woman has found a temporary home with me, but we shall see what Prince Adolphus makes of it when he knows the whole!'

The frozen look on Lottie's face brought an added glint of malice. 'You have naturally notified His Royal Highness of his daughter's disappearance?'

Lottie glanced at Prince Paul, who raised an interrogatory eyebrow.

'No,' she said reluctantly. 'I had hoped that we might find her before . . .'

'But he must be told!' Countess von Deiter did not trouble to hide her pleasure at Lottie's imminent downfall. 'He is her father as well as Gellenstadt's ruler – you cannot hope to keep such a tragic happening from him!'

'I am sure that the Baroness had no thought of trying to conceal the news from His Royal Highness indefinitely,' said von Gratz, smoothly sardonic. 'But how much more sympathetic Prince Adolphus will be if his daughter can be restored to him along with any confession of culpability! Am I not right, Baroness?'

Lottie swallowed the retort that sprang to her lips, but her eyes were overbright as she outstared them, head high.

'Enough!' said Prince Paul, his voice grating, and he took her arm and hurried her out to her carriage. 'She will be found!' he said, handing her up, but she could not see his face clearly for the tears that blinded her.

Back at the apartment, Josef had no news for her. 'But no news is perhaps better than bad news, Baroness,' he murmured in a clumsy but well-meaning desire to comfort.

Lottie could not settle anywhere. She felt so useless, and as she wandered from room to room the Countess' words beat in her head. Had she been over-casual in her dealings with Sophia? Prince Adolphus had placed his daughter in her care. If Sophia was . . . had come to any harm, how was she to break the news to him? 'I had a headache, sire, and permitted Sophia to go out without proper supervision.' Good God! How feeble it sounded!

She stood at last in the music room, staring bleakly at the finished portrait of Sophia. Eugene had done an excellent job. It was so lifelike – the proud little tilt of the head, the dreaminess in the dark eyes and a slight upward curve to the mouth that robbed the face of severity without detracting in any way from that Bayersdorf dignity.

She leaned her head against the chair back and wept.

Only gradually did she become aware of some kind of intense activity going on in the room beyond. As the sound registered, her immediate thought was for Sophia. They had found her!

She picked up her skirts and flew to the door. And there she met Josef on his way to find her.

'Is it . . .?' she cried.

'Baroness . . .' he began.

But already she was looking over his shoulder. Walking slowly across the salon to a chair, and looking so frail that she wondered how he stood at all, was Prince Adolphus. And behind him, her cane thumping with each step, came Her Serene Highness, the Dowager Princess Wilhelmina Louise.

13

In the dark depths of the cellar, Alys was the first to recover her wits. While Sophia clung to her, still fearful, her sobs turning to intermittent hiccups, Alys was listening, trying to establish some picture of where they were.

She had fumbled for and found the rug the men had tossed down after them, and it was now wrapped around them against the dankness as they sat huddled on the bottom step. 'At least they don't want us dead,' she said calmly, 'or they wouldn't have troubled to leave us this.'

'I'm sure there are rats,' Sophia whimpered. 'If only one might see something – *anything*, but this total blackness is so frightening!'

Alys laughed shakily – a brave but hollow sound in that place. 'Not for me, my dear.'

'Oh, I'm sorry. How unfeeling of me! I had not thought . . . this is how it must be for you all the time. How ever do you bear it?'

'Not always as well as I might,' Alys said wryly. 'But in this instance at least it does give me some small advantage. We may not know exactly where we are, or why – but I might be able to discover what kind of place this is, and even, if I am lucky, whether there might be some other way out.'

'You won't leave me?' Sophia cried out in sudden alarm.

'No, of course I won't. But we must make a plan. I thought perhaps I might find my way back up the steps first and bang on the door. You never know, someone might hear. And if that doesn't work, I'll explore my way around a little down here.' She felt the younger girl tense and added hurriedly, 'I think we should both sing. That way I should know all the time where you were and you would be able to hear me – and besides, it would keep our spirits up!'

'Well, if you think so . . .' Sophia wasn't sure she altogether liked the idea, but the merest possibility that they might find a way out was sufficient to bolster her courage.

Alys stood up and felt her way carefully up the steps holding on to the wall. The door at the top felt very solid and seemed to have no means of opening it that she could find. She banged and shouted, but her hands made little impression on the wood, and her voice sounded a mere puny echo fading away.

She went back down again and felt her way along the wall in the other direction while Sophia's thready voice quavered through a German folk song over and over again. Her boot kicked against something fairly solid and she stooped a little diffidently to see what it was. It proved to be a stout knobbly stick and she found it invaluable for feeling her way ahead. Presently she disturbed a small pile of rubble. Again she bent to investigate, and a shiver ran down her back. But she persevered and gradually became aware of a noise.

'Sophia – could you stop singing, just for a moment?'

Alys held her breath to listen. It was a distant booming sound, swelling and fading, and she realized almost at once what it was.

'I'm coming back,' she called, and carefully retraced her steps. 'I think,' she said, sitting down beside the younger girl and schooling her voice lest she should frighten her, 'that we are in the catacombs beneath one of the churches.' She felt Sophia shudder and hurried on. 'I'm almost sure that I heard an organ playing just now. Well, don't you see, my dear – if I'm right, there will be a way into them from the church!'

'Yes, but don't they have a lot of passages? We could get lost and wander round f-for ever . . .' Sophia fell silent and then said more calmly, 'I'm sorry. I am not behaving very well, am I?'

'Don't be silly.' Alys put her arm round her and they pulled the rug close round them. 'We'll stay here for a few minutes longer and I'll try the door again in case someone heard my calls and has gone for help. If nothing comes of that, we can begin to make our way towards the sound of the organ.'

Above them in the darkness, people occasionally hurried through the alleyway behind St Stefan's Cathedral on their way to brighter, safer places, carefully avoiding the body of a mongrel lying in a congealing pool of blood, and hearing nothing. But the faint call for help stirred the small spark of life still lingering inside the dog – and presently he lifted his head and whimpered.

It seemed to Lottie that for a moment they all stood like a tableau – unmoving. Then she was hurrying forward, saying all the proper things by force of habit while her mind seethed with problems and unanswered questions – the overriding one of all being, how was she to break the news to Prince Adolphus that his daughter was missing?

But amidst all the bustle as he and the Dowager Princess were settled near the fire, which had been allowed to burn low in all the upset and which a servant was hastily kindling into new life, her first consideration must be for their comfort. Josef was dispatched to arrange bedchambers and provide some light refreshment for the travellers.

'I don't understand, sire, how you come to be here?' she said, when at last the Prince's breathing had eased and he was looking less grey and pinched by the cold. 'Surely you should not have attempted such a journey at this time of year?'

'There was no help for it, my dear Charlotte.' Did she imagine more austerity than usual in his voice, or was it simply tiredness? 'There have been so many tiresome letters of late – from Count von Deiter and his wife – 'a decided chill here '– from Fräulein Lanner and von Gratz, not to mention your good self. So much confusion!'

He inclined his head towards his mother who sat bolt upright, her cold eyes missing nothing of Lottie's distress, the lingering trace of tears hastily wiped away, and his voice thinned even more.

'Her Serene Highness was finally resolved upon seeing for herself, and I really could not permit her to make the journey alone –'

'Fool's talk!' The cane rapped the floor. 'I have been making journeys all my life – more than you ever have! The plain fact is, Baroness, that we have been much disturbed to learn in our most recent correspondence about your deplorable treatment of Fräulein Lanner. Clearly you have exceeded the bounds of your authority in dismissing the Fräulein, who was in my opinion the one stabilizing influence in this household!'

'Mother!' sighed Prince Adolphus, with unutterable weariness.

'No use being mealy-mouthed about it! She disapproved of much that went on here – and was turned off for speaking her mind!'

Lottie could feel the familiar surge of frustration and anger rising in her. She said stiffly, 'Your Serene Highness has been misinformed. Fräulein Lanner was dismissed because she reduced Princess Sophia to a state of terror, the details of which I do not propose to go into at this time.' She could feel her voice rising, and stopped to draw breath before saying more calmly, as Josef came to signify that all was prepared, 'I am sure that both Your Highnesses are very tired. Could not the recriminations wait until morning?'

'Yes, indeed.' Prince Adolphus sounded relieved. He prepared to rise.

'As a matter of interest, where is Sophia?' asked the Grand Princess.

It was the question Lottie had been dreading. She had been trying to nerve herself to break the news, and even now she hardly knew how to begin.

'She is . . . not here,' she began.

Before she could elaborate the door burst open and Prince Paul strode in, his coat billowing, his easy manner for the moment abandoned. He stopped short.

'Good God! Adolphus? Mother?' He swung round to Lottie, who shook her head. 'I . . . they don't know yet,' she whispered, the strain showing in her voice.

Paul frowned and turned back to face the others. 'Sophia is missing,' he said with an absence of tact that at any other time she would have deplored. As a gleam of accusation came into his mother's eyes he added harshly, 'Baroness Lottie is in no way to blame.'

Lottie's concern was with Prince Adolphus, whose eyes had a blank shocked look. She flew to his side and knelt to chafe his hand.

'Please, sire, try not to worry! I'm sure she will be found very soon!'

Her Serene Highness' mouth was working. 'It is all of a piece with the rest!'

Prince Paul brushed aside her interruption.

'Lottie – I have come, to say that you were right, and I wish to God that I had acted upon your warnings sooner!'

From her place beside Prince Adolphus, she looked up at him and thought she had never seen him so serious, so devoid of mockery.

'I have been making inquiries, and twisting a few arms, and it transpires that the plot to abduct Sophia was hatched by Franz, abetted by Countess von Deiter.' He swore softly. 'I was so sure I had their measure!'

A small hiss of indrawn breath from the Dowager Princess made him look towards her. 'I'm sorry, dear Mama, but your informant in chief has been dirtying her hands. I don't know how far the Count is involved – but I doubt he has the brains or the stomach for such an enterprise!'

'Paul, will you kindly explain what all this is about?' Against the leaping firelight Prince Adolphus' profile was etched with a skeletal starkness that emphasized his unspoken fear, but his voice, though thready with weariness, was firm.

Paul moved to the fireplace and stood, head bowed, hand resting on the mantel shelf. For a long moment he stared down into the flames as though gathering his courage. Then he turned to face them.

'Full explanations will have to wait. For now, all that matters is that Franz von Gratz has conspired to have Sophia and the friend who was with her held somewhere in safekeeping – ' Paul saw the raw agony in his brother's eyes and reiterated harshly, '*In safekeeping*.'

'Can you guarantee me that?' Adolphus asked, his voice low.

'No – but I'd stake my life on it.'

'I see,' came the bleak reply.

'No! Oh God, you don't see at all!' Paul exclaimed, as though driven. 'Believe me, I'm not exactly proud of my part in all this, unwitting though it was. I admit that initially I supported Franz's suit – I saw in it all kinds of advantages for the future – for the future of Gellenstadt.' There was defiance in his eyes as they met his brother's. 'But of late my views have begun to change.' His glance at Lottie was full of bitter self-mockery. 'You might say I was brought to see the error of my ways! Also, I became rather fond of my niece – too fond to see her wed to Franz.'

He brought his fist down on the nearby table with a force that made everyone jump. 'I should have guessed that when you rejected his offer, he wouldn't leave it there! He took the whole thing too damned calmly after his initial outburst. He must have begun plotting almost at once – and Irena von Deiter, seduced by promises of advancement for her husband, became his willing ally.'

'But how was it accomplished?' Lottie asked, hating to see him so full of self-blame.

'With the greatest ease.' Paul's mouth twisted. 'She knew that Enghein's sister had asked Sophia to take tea – at the time it was thought that you would be going also – an added bonus to see you brought low.' He frowned, and then continued, 'It was she who arranged for the note of apology to be delivered.'

'But the coach?'

'An acquaintance of Franz, considerably in debt to him, was *persuaded* to loan him the coach. In appearance it was not unlike the one you were expecting. A couple of thugs to carry out the deed, and all was set in motion.'

His mother had been sitting rigidly erect, as though holding herself together by force. 'This is pure make-believe! You had ever a fertile imagination, Paul.' She thumped the floor with her cane. 'What possible motive could Duke von Gratz have had for devising such an unlikely scheme?'

This had vexed Lottie's mind, too – though she believed every word.

'The simplest of all motives, mother dear – to earn the gratitude of a grieving father. It doesn't take too much imagination to guess at that father's feelings when his daughter is rescued and returned to him by the rejected suitor who has proved himself by scouring the city in order that he might with great unselfishness restore the girl to safety.' Paul glanced at his brother and said with deep irony, 'Even you, brother dear, would find your heart softening towards such a one, am I not right?'

'Perhaps.' The Prince's voice was dour. 'In which case, might it not behove you to find her first?'

'My pardon.' There was bitterness in Paul's sardonic acknowledgement. 'It is my intention. I had thought I had made a fair beginning!'

'Oh, you have!' Lottie cried, feeling his hurt – and unaware how much her defence of him betrayed her.

Paul gave her a queer little smile. 'Don't grieve for me, lovely Lottie. I never did learn the knack of pleasing my big brother!'

The door burst open yet again to admit Max. He bowed hurriedly to Sophia's family. 'My apologies,' he exclaimed as Lottie made him known, 'but I thought you would wish to know – '

'You have found them!' Lottie cried.

'No, but we have found that dog, and I believe he may know where they are. Ferdie has him downstairs. The animal has been quite badly hurt, but he won't let either of us near him . . . keeps whining and running away as though he wants us to follow.'

'Then what are we waiting for?' Paul said.

'I'll get a cloak.' Lottie almost ran towards the door.

Paul stopped her. 'No, you won't. You have duties to perform here.'

Her shoulders sagged, and Max put an arm round them. 'Don't fret, my dear. We'll bring them safely back, I promise you.'

The three men with the dog loping ahead of them exchanged few words until they came within sight of the Cathedral.

'I suppose this animal does know where it's going?' Prince Paul said tersely.

'He knows,' Ferdie replied.

The dog skirted the Stefans platz, loping in the shadows, and then, as though sensing that his goal was in sight, he increased his stride. Max signed to his coachman, who had been keeping pace with them, to wait in the square, and they hurried after the dog.

In a dim passageway behind the Cathedral he stopped and began to paw urgently at the wall. Ferdie, who had had the presence of mind to bring a lantern, shone it closer and they saw a door with heavy wooden bars slotting into the wall top and bottom. In no time they had it open and the dog immediately vanished down the flight of worn stone steps. They called, but there was silence, except for the animal's sharp questing barks.

'A damned fool's errand, belike!' Paul's voice was impatient, but there was a trembling insistence in Max's 'No!'

'We can only trust the dog,' Ferdie insisted stubbornly, and began to descend. At the bottom they found another door opening on to a passage.

'My God – catacombs!' he groaned, as the light flickered over the alcoves with their grisly relics. 'What inhuman monster would bring the girls here? These tunnels are like a warren – they run for miles in all directions. If Alys and the Princess have wandered off . . .' He left the sentence unfinished, but the same dread was in all their minds, leaving them in a black despair.

When shouting brought only the mocking echoes of their own voices, the three began the unenviable task of devising the best way of making a systematic search of the place. The argument grew quite heated so that they did not immediately hear the dog's excited yelps.

'Be silent!' Paul snapped. The sound seemed to come from all sides. 'Oh God! Which way?'

'It is here!' cried Ferdie and plunged into the darkness, taking the lantern so that they were forced to follow him. The barking grew louder and then there were voices – blessedly feminine voices. They broke into a run, and a moment later Sophia and Alys with their arms round the ecstatic mongrel, laughing and crying and almost squeezing the life out of him.

'Oh, we are so g-glad to see you!' Sophia sobbed into Paul's coat as he lifted her in his arms, while Max and Ferdie between them supported Alys. 'Alys has b-been quite splendid . . . much braver than me!'

'Nonsense!' Alys explained about hearing the organ and her confidence that there must be a church nearby. As the three men exchanged glances, Max took from her the greyish white object she had been using for a stick and tossed it into an alcove with the other bones.

Soon the girls were back home and tucked up in bed, Sophia having first to endure a confrontation with her father and, more dauntingly, her grandmother, both of whom had insisted upon waiting up. However, Lottie in a surge of relief, insisted that the child was exhausted and all questions must wait until morning. And such was her authority that even the Dowager Princess was silenced.

'What will you do about Franz von Gratz?' she asked Paul as he was leaving.

'I shall deal with him, of course.'

His voice sounded so strange that Lottie found herself clutching at his arm. 'You won't do anything stupid?'

He stared at her hand for a moment, then removed it and lifted it to his lips. 'Would you grieve for me, *Liebling*?' he asked with the ghost of a smile, his eyes on hers. 'Why, I do believe you would! Of course, it is more than likely that my earlier investigations will have alerted him, in which case he will have gone to ground.' His voice grew silky. 'However, I can be amazingly patient when I have to be.'

Max too was anxious to settle with von Gratz, and did not take kindly to Prince Paul's assumption of that prerogative. 'Alys is my sister,' he insisted. 'I have the right.'

'And Sophia is my niece,' Paul said softly. 'And heir to the throne of my country. Also, Franz abused our friendship, and that gives me the edge, don't you think?'

In the end they both kept watch at the entrance to the catacombs, but nothing happened. Nor did Franz return to Am Hof, so they were obliged to conclude that he had fled Vienna.

Count and Countess von Deiter also left hurriedly, after a brief and painful interview with Prince Adolphus in which they were ordered home to pack their belongings before leaving Gellenstadt for good.

The girls recovered remarkably quickly from their ordeal, and the valiant Fidelio, his wounds salved, was made much of – being treated to all manner of delicacies, and fussed over with anxious solicitude by Tasha – all of which he accepted placidly as his duc.

Lottie's main concern now was for Prince Adolphus, who was confined to his bed for several days following upon the rigours of the journey culminating in the shock that he suffered at the end of it. The finest doctors in Vienna – as recommended by Prince Metternich – were summoned, and prescribed rest, together with various sedatives and potions.

Sophia, rather to everyone's surprise, spent much of her time sitting with him, for though recovered, she was disinclined to resume her former carefree existence. Lottie was pleased that father and daughter were at last getting to know one another rather better, though it did leave her with the less happy task of keeping the Dowager Princess amused.

Any hope that her advanced age might confine her to her room for long periods was soon dispelled; now that she was here in Vienna, she clearly intended to make the most of her time. Her disapproval of Lottie did not noticeably diminish, but she was presently obliged to acknowledge that her circle of friends, some of them quite intimate, could hardly be faulted, and in the wake of Sophia's ordeal, the quantity of flowers and good wishes and the number of callers who came to commiserate and console were certainly most gratifying. Count Enghein's pink roses alone filled the whole of one corner of the salon and brought a soft matching colour to Sophia's cheeks.

'I believe the old dragon is impressed,' Lottie told Alexei one afternoon as they watched Her Serene Highness holding court in the salon, and conversing almost amiably with Prince Talleyrand and his niece, Madame Eduard de Périgord. 'But she will never admit it!'

'So? If it is her pleasure to think ill of you let her.' He grinned. 'We, your dear friends, value you as you should be valued, and that is all that matters. Have you and Max set a date for your marriage yet?'

It was a casual question, but he observed with little surprise that she was slow to answer, as though it was receiving much more thought than it merited, and when she *did* answer, her eyes did not quite meet his.

'Oh, well – with all the upset, you know, there has been hardly any time to discuss it. And besides, Alys must have her moment of happiness first. It would be unfair to deprive her of any of the excitement that surrounds such a momentous occasion.'

It was a pretty speech, the very epitome of unselfishness – except that he did not for one moment believe that there was not much more to it. She did not sound at all as a woman in love should sound when obliged to wait for fulfilment. But he held his peace.

*

Perhaps it was the advent of the Duke of Wellington, or maybe the first faint hint of spring in the air – but the festivities which had begun to flag were suddenly resumed with renewed vigour. A masquerade ball was to be given by Prince Metternich in the Duke of Wellington's honour – and everyone threw themselves into the preparations as though it were the first event of its kind; costumes of medieval splendour, uniforms covered in embroidery and braided in silver and gold, vied here and there with dominoes of every hue, and masks were anything from a slip of black silk to the most extravagant lace creations. And in Prince Metternich's house on the Ballplatz on the night of the ball the music and the laughter seemed set to continue until dawn

The event marked Sophia's first formal appearance since her misfortune and Lottie wanted it to be special for her – to erase from her mind the events of that dreadful day. She therefore took particular care with her gown, which consisted of a long loose tunic of palest pink over a petticoat of white satin, fastened all the way down with tiny pearls. The bodice was decorated also with pearls and it had wide floating sleeves, with under-sleeves of white satin. Lottie's own gown was similar in design, but her tunic was of a rich blue and where she wore a little jewelled toque, Sophia's headdress came to a delicate point from which floated a long gossamer veil, which she carried with pride.

'You have done well, Charlotte,' said Prince Adolphus, surveying his daughter with obvious pleasure. 'I wouldn't have believed how well she has turned out,' he added when Sophia had left the room.

'Thank you, sire,' she said, dimpling. 'I always said she would.'

'So you did.'

'All she needs now is time,' Lottie added with great daring. 'I would not have her rushed into anything.'

He sighed, and she immediately wished the words unsaid, for although he was well enough now to leave his bed, no miracles had been performed.

'Well, we shall see,' he said, his eyes resting on her with such a look of yearning that she could hardly bear to withstand it. 'What a fool I was!' he said enigmatically.

The Dowager Princess had elected to attend the ball. She entered the ballroom as though it was exactly where she belonged, gowned in black velvet encrusted with jewels, her cane defiantly tapping the floor, a glittering diadem at odds with the wrinkled face which scorned a mask.

'You have to hand it to Mama,' murmured Paul. 'She can still make an entrance!'

And Lottie could not but agree.

It was after supper, when they were leaving the salon where the superb collation was laid out, that Lottie became momentarily separated from Max and found her way impeded by a colossus in a wine-coloured domino.

When he made no immediate attempt to get out of her way, she said good-humouredly, 'Pray allow me to pass, sir.'

For answer, he took her arm in a bruising grip and turned her away from the ballroom, and at the same moment she felt something sharp pressing hard into her side.

'Do not make any noise, Baroness,' said Franz von Gratz softly. 'We are just going for a little private settling of scores, you and I.'

14

'Forgive me, Your Highness, but have you seen Baroness Lottie?'

Even now Max could not bring himself to be anything less than formal with Prince Paul – and from the sardonic look in the Prince's eyes, he was very much aware of the fact.

'We had just come from the supper room, and one moment she was with me and the next she was gone,' he explained.

Paul shrugged. 'Perhaps you should take better care of her, Annesley. You may yet lose her for good,' he drawled. He saw the faint colour come up under Mr Annesley's skin, as it stretched taut across the classic nose and mouth. And he cursed silently. 'You could try the ballroom,' he added carelessly. 'Metlin has probably carried her off to dance.'

Max nodded abruptly. 'My thanks, I'll do that.'

Paul presently wandered into the ballroom himself. The orchestra had just struck up for a polonaise, and he saw that Prince Metlin was indeed at the head of the dancers as they marched off. But he had Sophia for partner, not Lottie. He put up his glass and looked along the line. No Lottie.

Mildly curious, he strolled the length of the ballroom and came at last to the small dais where the dowagers were seated, his mother among them like a small imperious crow amid a flock of plump pigeons. She saw him and beckoned imperatively.

'Who is that dancing with Sophia?' she demanded.

He told her, and she proceeded to quizz him about Metlin.

'My dear mother, you give me credit for more interest than I can claim. I know little of Metlin's background, and care less, but he is an amiable enough fellow. A shocking flirt, though,' he added with gentle malice.

Paul watched the interested appraisal in his mother's eyes turn to disapproval. She put up her lorgnette.

'The child is too familiar with him. I shall speak to her.' The Princess' voice sharpened. 'Where is the Baroness? Why is she not watching more closely how the child conducts herself? In view of recent events, one would expect that she would be more rather than less vigilant!'

'Perhaps she has noted how well you do her job for her,' Paul drawled. And then, impatiently, 'rest easy, Mama! Alexei Metlin is no Franz. Sophia will come to no harm there.'

He moved away before she could involve him in any tiresome duties, and resolved to find Lottie for himself. Before he had gone far, however, he found himself being hailed by the Duke of Wellington, who remembered him from Peninsular days and one particular engagement in which he had distinguished himself.

'This is all a little different, what?' he said with that neighing laugh that Paul remembered so well. 'But I am hopeful of being able to bring matters to a speedy conclusion. Castlereagh has done most of the work, thanks be! Alexander seems well pleased with his Polish acquisitions – and so he should be! And Prussia is to have two-fifths of Saxony.' He shook his head. 'Everyone greedy for power. There is still Murat to deal with in Italy, of course, and the German settlements – that is your interest, I suppose.'

Paul schooled himself to converse politely, but something of his restlessness must have communicated itself, for Wellington finally said with a chuckle, 'But there, I mustn't keep you from the ladies, what?' and moved on.

When Paul at last found Max Annesley in one of the anterooms, still looking for Lottie, a vague disquiet settled upon him; with no basis in reason, it yet lay like a stone within his chest.

'This is ridiculous,' Max said. 'Cousin Carrie has just come from the room reserved for the ladies, and she isn't there.'

Paul turned without a word and strode swiftly to the entrance hall. '*You.*' He beckoned some of the flunkeys. 'Have you seen a young lady in a blue gown?' He described Lottie briefly.

The servant looked apprehensive, as though blame might somehow attach to him. 'Would the lady be with a large gentleman wearing a domino . . . a wine-coloured domino, I believe?' The look in his interrogator's eyes made him even more nervous. 'Such a couple did leave . . . maybe ten minutes since.'

Paul flung round to stare at Max, and though his manner was restrained, there was a wild glittering urgency in his eyes that almost caused Max to flinch. 'Did you notice this man in the wine-coloured domino?' Paul's voice grated.

'No . . . at least, there are so many . . .'

But Paul was already turning back to the flunkey, firing questions at him. 'How did they leave . . . by coach . . . on foot? Did you see which way they went?'

The man grew flustered. It was not his duty to summon the coach, but another servant's.

'Bring him to me.'

Hurriedly the man was summoned and interrogated just as tersely, but with more success. Yes, the couple had left in a coach – very close, they had seemed – and in a hurry, for the lady was not wearing her cloak. The coach had taken the Schönbrunn road.

'Then I know where they've gone,' Paul said, and demanded his coach on the instant.

'No doubt you will explain when you see fit, Highness,' Max said stiffly, as Paul paced impatiently until the coach arrived. 'Meanwhile, wherever you are going I insist upon accompanying you. If Lottie's safety and honour are at risk then I –'

Paul turned on him viciously. '*She is mine, Annesley*! She may be betrothed to you, but she has always been mine!'

There was so much anguish in the Prince's voice that the hot denial which sprang to Max's lips remained unspoken. Instead, he said quietly, 'That, Highness, is surely for Lottie to decide. For the moment the pressing need must be to ensure her safety, and as I *am* her fiancé, you cannot deny me the right to involve myself.'

'Oh, very well. Come if you must!' Paul snapped. 'But don't get in my way!'

They were in the coach and rattling over the ground at a most alarming speed before Max ventured to pursue the question of where they were going and why. The answer came swiftly.

'There is a hunting lodge out on the Schönbrunn road. Please God, that's where he has taken her!'

'You *are* speaking of Franz von Gratz, of course?'

'Well, who else do you know who would attempt anything so insane?' Prince Paul moved restively and in the flicker of the swaying carriage lights his eyes glowed like coals. 'I should have realized,' he muttered, half to himself. 'Franz blamed Lottie for the rejection of his suit . . . when Adolphus' letter came he was almost hysterical in his rage. That was when I began to see how ruthless and single-minded he had become.'

It hardly seemed the moment, but the question had to be put. 'And if you are wrong about where he has taken her?'

There was a silence in which the rattling of the coach wheels sounded like thunder. 'Then, God help me, I shall have failed her!' he said, his voice sunk to a whisper.

Max said no more, but his thoughts were sombre in the extreme.

The coach swung into a drive and pulled up at the foot of a short flight of steps. Paul was out before it had stopped and was pealing on the bell. The door opened no more than a crack.

'Your Highness?' The elderly servant sounded startled; also he looked frightened.

'Where are they?' Paul rapped the words out.

The manservant shrunk a little, opened the door wider and indicated the room at the rear that he and Lottie had used on that previous occasion.

Lottie was cold and frightened, and tense with the efforts of holding off the moment when Franz von Gratz would end his game of cat and mouse which he had sadistically pursued from the moment he had forced her to leave Prince Metternich's house at knifepoint.

During the short journey he had made conversation in a formal polite way that was so completely at odds with what he was saying that it seemed twice as unnerving, and lest she might entertain any ideas about escape, the knife continued to prod her, punctuating the more salient points of his discourse.

'I have wanted you for years, did you know that? Ever since I came to Gellenstadt that time and you were there – married to that ageing aesthetic! Such a waste, I thought . . . all that unsullied purity – ' She moved to protest and the knife pricked sharply. 'It was unsullied, wasn't it? I would have enjoyed you then, but I'm glad now that the pleasure is still before me. You are so much *riper* now than you were in those days!'

Lottie felt sick, but she knew that her only hope lay in allowing him to pursue his vile one-sided conversation, in the hope that somehow a means of escape would offer itself.

'It would have been so much simpler to bring you to heel once I was married to Princess Sophia. You really shouldn't have baulked my chances there . . . I shall have to teach you to pay more heed to me!' He laughed as an involuntary shudder ran through her. 'Frightened, are you?'

'I am cold,' she said through her chattering teeth.

'Content yourself, you will soon be much warmer!'

She did not immediately recognize the house when they arrived; only when the manservant let them in did she remember, though he showed no sign of recognizing her; in any case he was clearly too frail to be of the least help.

Von Gratz hurried her through to the back room and closed the door with an awful finality. There was a fire that gave out little warmth, and a table laid with food and wine. He flung off the domino and poured two glasses of wine, putting one into her hand.

'Drink,' he said, tossing back his own.

'I don't want it,' she retorted, setting the glass down.

He picked it up and closed her fingers round it, then thrust it against her lips, his other hand hard beneath her chin.

'Drink!'

She complied, warned by the look in his eyes. At first she had supposed him to be more than a little drunk, but now she wondered if it was not rather a kind of unnatural excitement that filled him. He was enjoying himself in a way that disgusted her, and her fear grew.

'I should like something to eat,' she said desperately.

'Why not?' He pulled out a chair for her with exaggerated courtesy and sat down opposite her. Every mouthful of food was an effort, but she persisted, dragging the meal out for as long as she could, averting her eyes from von Gratz as he consumed everything before him with relish, replenishing his glass frequently and urging her to drink.

'It will sustain you,' he said, and laughed, biting into a peach and wiping the juice from his chin with the back of his hand.

At last even he was replete and she knew that there was no possible way that she could hold him off any longer – nothing she could use to defend herself. He rose and walked towards her. She scraped her chair back and retreated until the back of a sofa brought her to an abrupt halt. With a feeling of terror she saw that he had the knife in his hand once more.

'Now,' he said, and as she arched back instinctively, not knowing what to expect, he sliced through the fastenings down the front of her tunic. The jewelled buttons flew off, scattering across the floor like hailstones, and her white satin petticoat billowed free.

Lottie cried out, and wasn't aware of the door opening until Paul's voice, awful in its fury, came as an unbelievable answer to her cry. He was there, framed in the doorway with Max close behind him, and as von Gratz turned with the knife still in his raised hand, it seemed that he was about to hurl it at Paul. She clutched at his arm, reaching up in an attempt to seize it. With a shout of rage he shook her off, pushing her violently so that she fell, striking her head against the table.

Paul was across the room almost before she hit the ground and, catching Franz still off-balance, felled him with a single bone-jarring blow.

With contemptuous indifference he turned his back on him and ran to Lottie. Max was already bending over her, but Paul pushed him aside.

'Leave her to me!' he cried hoarsely, catching her up in his arms. '*Liebling*?' And as she moaned and began to stir, 'Oh my love, my dear love, you are safe now. Hush!' He cradled her close, and said over his shoulder and in a voice that shook slightly, 'Annesley, be so good as to go out to the coach and ask my man for my pistols.'

Max had watched the scene being enacted before him as though it were some kind of bad dream. But this pulled him up.

'Are you run mad?' he exclaimed. 'Good God, the man is out cold! You can't mean to shoot him?'

'I shall naturally wait until he comes to his senses,' Paul said with a careless want of concern. 'Do as I ask, there's a good fellow.'

Max shook his head and went out.

Paul lifted Lottie in his arms and laid her gently on the sofa.

He examined the contusion on the side of her head and sighed. 'Poor *Liebling*. But it could be worse, though you'll feel it for a day or two.'

Lottie felt sick and dizzy and quite unequal to any kind of coherent thought, but as his face swam before her, she saw the love blazing in his eyes as she had never seen it before, and such gentleness.

'Oh!' she whispered wonderingly, and then her eyelids became too heavy and fluttered down.

When Franz von Gratz returned to consciousness, it was to find Prince Paul standing over him, his face quite devoid of expression, a pistol cradled almost negligently in one hand, aimed in his direction.

He explored his chin with shaking fingers. 'I think you have broken my jaw,' he muttered.

'It can hardly matter since I intend to kill you anyway,' Paul said.

He spoke so matter of factly that the words did not at first sink in. But the pistol was real enough. Franz scrambled to his feet, eyeing it warily.

'In cold blood?' he sneered. 'Is it then to be an execution?' But his eyes were shifting about the room, noting Max near the sofa, the closed door, his knife lying out of reach on the floor, and the table already moved out of the way.

Paul watched him dispassionately. 'Oh, I'll give you a sporting chance, little as you deserve it, but the end will be the same.'

'Can you be sure of that?' Franz was blustering, unable to accept the possibility of defeat. 'I gave you that scar, remember – when you were eighteen?' He saw that his words were having little effect. 'Ah, look now, Paul, be sensible. We're friends – and friends don't kill one another – not over a woman . . .'

The hammer of Paul's pistol clicked back. 'Pick it up.' He indicated the other one lying on the table. His voice was menacing in its softness. 'Now – or I shoot you where you stand!'

He moved away, watching Franz do as he was bid, watching him every inch of the way, not trusting him as he went through the motions of balancing the pistol. He cocked the hammer and half-turned.

'A few steps further back, I think,' Paul said. 'Annesley – be so good as to drop your handkerchief, if you please, when you are ready.'

Max recognized that they were both beyond reason and reluctantly complied. But von Gratz panicked and fired a fraction early.

Prince Paul felt the searing impact even as he saw his own bullet sink into Franz's chest, and both men fell together. The explosion of sound brought Lottie back to consciousness. She sat up, gasped aloud as the pain shot through her head, causing a momentary giddiness. Then she saw Paul lying motionless with Max already stooping to examine his arm where a rent in his coat was seeping blood. She spared no more than a brief glance for von Gratz, before running crazily, unsteadily to Paul and falling on her knees beside him – tears streaming down her face as she sobbed his name over and over.

Max reassured her in an expressionless voice that it was only a flesh wound, and moved aside to contemplate the ruins of more than the outcome of the duel.

Paul was very still, his face pale and wiped clean of all expression. Lottie wanted to shake him, to make him speak to her, her own aching head forgotten in her need to bring him back so that she might see again that love blazing in his eyes. Her tears fell unheeded on his face.

'Oh, please, Paul!' she whispered. 'Please wake up – I love you . . . I need you!'

Without warning, his good arm came up to pull her down on top of him, and his mouth was finding hers, devouring her with a need that was the culmination of all the worry and danger and sheer fright of the past hours, and she no longer holding back, pressed closer, clinging to him as though she would never let him go, until at last they fell apart, crying with relief and wincing with pain at the same time.

'Oh!' she cried, pummelling his chest with her fist. 'Beast! To let me think that you were . . .'

He imprisoned her fist in his good hand. 'Pax!' he implored. 'You wouldn't strike an injured man!' and immediately she was all solicitude again, and insisted that she must wash and bind his wound.

Max turned away, unable to bear their intimacy a moment

longer. He went to look at von Gratz who was quite obviously dead, and wearily he bent to pick up the discarded pistols. The air reeked with the smell of burned powder.

Behind him, Lottie was the first to come back to some kind of sanity. She saw him, saw the disconsolate droop of his shoulders, and the tears of weakness filled her eyes again. She left Paul and walked slowly across the room.

'Max?' She touched his arm. 'My dear, I'm so sorry . . .'

He smiled at her, a resigned subdued kind of smile, meant to reassure. 'It's all right, my dear girl. I think I have known all along, but I didn't want to admit it.'

'I am so very fond of you – '

'Please!' he said abruptly. 'Not now. Later, perhaps, but not now!'

Paul, too, had risen and came to stand with them, his arm resting with casual intimacy around Lottie's shoulder. He looked down at Franz and said with a sudden anger, 'Oh, the devil take it, why did he have to be such a *fool*?'

15

That repercussions would follow the events of that night seemed inevitable. A duel, however ably hushed up, could hardly be expected to pass without comment. Disquiet was expressed in court circles and Emperor Francis let it be known that the affair had incurred his extreme displeasure, but in view of the special mitigating circumstances surrounding the whole business, no further action was deemed necessary.

'I suppose I should not be surprised to find you making scandals,' Prince Adolphus had said austerely when confronted by his brother looking pale and dishevelled, and with his arm supported by a swathe of linen. 'Did you *have* to kill von Gratz?'

'Would you rather I had left him free to ravish Lottie?' Paul returned, his voice grating.

The morning sunlight threw up the strong lines in the faces of both men, each weary and each in their own way full of righteous anger. Adolphus closed his eyes briefly.

'No, of course not,' he said at last. 'Is she much distressed?'

Paul's mouth twisted. 'I haven't seen her this morning but she will undoubtedly be nursing a sore head, and has been scared half out of her wits.' He looked Adolphus full in the eye. 'How do you *suppose* she will feel?' he said viciously.

Prince Adolphus stiffened against his pillows, his breath rasping. 'You have made your point. Forgive me if I sounded uncaring.' A spasm of distress crossed his face. 'You can have no idea what it is like to feel so *damnably* helpless!'

The admission, so totally unexpected, went a long way towards disarming Paul's hostility. It was the first time his brother had ever shown any weakness in his presence. Clumsily, one-handedly, he poured some cordial.

'Here,' he said awkwardly. 'Drink it. I shouldn't have troubled you with all this.'

'No, you were right to do so. I had rather be prepared.' Adolphus sipped the drink. 'Mother will hear of it soon enough. She came home last night with Sophia, not best pleased at having been deserted by you all, as she put it.' They exchanged a wry knowing smile. 'Poor Lottie, I fear she will once again bear the brunt, whatever may be said to exonerate her!'

'Well, she had better not accuse Lottie in my hearing,' Paul snapped, and encountered a frowning glance from his brother which he met with a careless shrug. 'I may as well tell you the whole,' he said. 'I intend to marry Lottie.'

For a moment there was no sound but the rasp of Prince Adolphus' breathing. Then: 'Strange, but I had gained the distinct impression that she was already spoken for?'

'Oh, that was just a stupid mistake.'

'I see.' Adolphus' voice was dry in the extreme. 'I take it Charlotte is aware that you propose to do her this great honour?'

Paul grinned, looking suddenly almost carefree. 'She knows!'

'And you are not, I trust, likely to be called to account to Mr Annesley for your presumption? A second duel so soon might take rather more explaining!'

'You needn't worry about Annesley. He has relinquished all claims to Lottie's affections.'

'Well, then.' Adolphus set the glass down carefully on the table beside his bed. 'I naturally rejoice that Charlotte is to become one of the family, though I fear that her wits must have gone a-begging.' As his brother grinned yet again and turned to leave, he added with sudden urgency, 'Paul – you had better make her happy . . .'

Something in his brother's voice made Paul look more closely at him. Just for an instant the austere face quivered with raw emotion. Then it was pulled taut, and only the overbright eyes betrayed Adolphus. Paul strode back to the bed and held out his good hand. 'My promise on it,' he said.

Adolphus felt the strong clasp and knew the bitter finality of lost dreams. Then he nodded abruptly – and let him go.

Any qualms that remained were set at rest by Charlotte herself. The faint shadow of her recent experience was evident, but when she spoke of Paul her eyes shone.

'I know that you haven't always trusted him, but he truly does care about Gellenstadt,' she told him eagerly. 'In fact, I have been wondering . . .'

Adolphus was regarding her so acutely that she blushed. 'Well, now that you have no Secretary of State . . .' He frowned and she hurried on. 'Paul would do the job splendidly, and I should be there to see that he didn't get carried away – and then Sophia would have time to grow up properly and not be rushed into marriage before she is ready . . .'

She was running on too much. She knew it. And he knew it!

'In fact, my dear Charlotte, you have arranged everything entirely as you feel it should be!'

She was not deceived by the severity of his voice. 'I'm sure it would work,' she said meekly.

'Very likely,' he said. 'Would you care to tell Mother – or shall I?'

As expected, the Dowager Princess had not taken kindly to the idea of Lottie becoming her daughter-in-law. She regarded her as a disruptive influence, and the combination of herself and Paul as nothing short of disastrous. 'The truth being,' said Paul with rare perception, 'that she knows only too well that she can't effectively browbeat either of us!'

Sophia was overjoyed at the news. The prospect of losing Lottie which had hung over her since her engagement to Max was not only removed, but she would now be able to claim her for an aunt.

'Of course, I am very sorry for Mr Annesley,' she added belatedly. 'To lose, first Alys and now you must be awful for him. Do you suppose that he knows how everyone is talking about him?'

'He knows,' Lottie said shortly, uncomfortably aware of the feelings of guilt that beset her whenever she remembered how shabbily she had treated Max. There had been a rather awkward few days when Alys seemed to be avoiding her and even Mrs Osmond regarded her with cool reproach and was less disposed than usual to chatter.

It was Max himself who had made matters right in the end. They met on the landing one morning, and he greeted her with scrupulous politeness as he had done on the only other occasion their paths had crossed. At first it seemed that he would pass on as before, then as she sought desperately for something to say, he hesitated and turned back.

'Lottie?'

'Yes?' she said eagerly.

'Oh, dammit, this is ridiculous!' he exclaimed. 'I can't hate you . . . if I'm honest, I can't even blame you. I knew in my heart from the first that you were in love with Prince Paul!'

'Did you?' Lottie said, momentarily diverted. 'How clever of you. I didn't!' And then, laying her hand on his arm, 'Max, I am so sorry!'

He covered her hand fleetingly with his own. 'Well, don't be. I shall come about, never fear.' He released her and said in practical tones, 'I have a favour to ask.'

'Anything,' she said.

'I shall be going home almost immediately after Alys' wedding. Cousin Carrie comes with me. I know she is very torn, but it is for the best. Ferdie has found an admirable girl to look after Alys – she is from a good family and speaks English surprisingly well – and it will be much better for Alys to have someone young about her.' Max hesitated. 'I don't know where you will be living when you are married, but I would be more than grateful if you would keep in touch with Alys – and perhaps let me know from time to time how she goes on.'

'Oh, my dear, of course I will! I should be very distressed indeed if what has happened were to come between us. Please tell her how sorry I am, and that I don't blame her in the least for being angry with me, but if she can bring herself to forgive me . . .'

Exactly what Max told his sister Lottie wasn't sure, but it had the required effect. Within a very short space of time the two young women were in one another's arms, laughing and crying – and all was mended.

Alys was to be married in mid-March. The last minute preparations were in full swing when Alexei arrived one morning bursting with news.

'Boney has escaped!' he exclaimed. 'Slipped out of Elba while no one was looking. You should just see what a state everyone is in, not knowing where he'll make for! There are messengers rushing back and forth between the embassies . . . it is all highly diverting!'

His complete irreverence helped to lessen the initial impact of the news, but when he had gone a mood of apprehension crept in.

'I suppose it will mean an end to all the parties and balls,' Sophia said a little wistfully.

When they went out later, however, to help Alys to put a few finishing touches to her little house, there was no evidence of panic – indeed it seemed at first glance that nothing had changed. Everywhere people were out in the spring sunshine, driving or strolling towards the Prater with every appearance of enjoyment – and an amateur performance of the *Barbier de Seville* to be given that evening at the Imperial Palace proceeded without any evidence of panic – though everyone was discussing the news and hazarding guesses as to where Napoleon would make for.

But behind the scenes the allied ministers were already busy. Intensive efforts were being made to reshape and conclude the various agreements which had been argued over in such a vacuous way for months. And when it became certain that Napoleon was on French soil and making for Paris in triumph, a joint declaration was issued by the Allies proclaiming that Napoleon Bonaparte had exposed himself to public indictment, and offering the King of France whatever assistance he needed to re-establish a state of tranquillity while disbanding armies were hastily regrouped.

The effect of this declaration upon Vienna and its merrymakers was insidious; people still danced and played, but now a tremor of apprehension ran beneath the gaiety and, like brilliant ephemeral bubbles, the balls and entertainments began to melt away one by one into the empty air.

Nothing, however, could mar Alys' wedding. She was married in the lovely church of Maria am Gestade close by the Danube canal and Ferdie had composed music specially for the ceremony. Alys in palest blue looked radiantly happy with her Ferdie, and Max was quietly proud, while Mrs Osmond cried continuously throughout.

The celebrations went on well into the night and when they had taken Sophia back to the apartment, Paul asked Lottie to go out with him again.

'But it's almost morning!' she said, laughing at him.

'So? Why don't we go up into the hills and watch the dawn come up?'

Lottie's eyes sparkled. 'Oh yes!'

'Go and change then, and we'll ride up.'

It was cold and clear as they left the city and allowed the horses to pick their own way up through the trees. They spoke very little, but Lottie felt that they had never been more in harmony.

Halfway up, they secured the horses and strolled along, holding hands. 'I feel about seventeen,' Lottie sighed happily.

'I'm glad you're not,' he murmured.

At the top of the ridge they turned to look back. A mist had drifted in over the city but here above it, all was still clear. Paul's arm was about her and she turned into him and lifted her face to him.

'Lovely, lovely Lottie! I still can't believe you are mine.' His mouth was warm and urgent and he pulled her down onto the carpet of soft spring heather. The beating of her heart almost suffocated her as he loosened the fastenings of her jacket and let his lips trail down until they came to rest in the curve of her breasts. Her whole body was melting into an indescribable sweetness. 'Dear God!' he said, his voice muffled. 'I do love you, *Liebling*!'

Her arms were round him and she was almost lost to everything. Then, reluctantly, he sat up. 'I think we had better be married very soon.'

'As soon as you like,' she said huskily. 'But your brother talks of going home. It would please him, I think, if we could be married there?'

He stood up and pulled her to her feet. 'Then let us please him, by all means,' he said and for once there was no sarcasm in his voice.

A faint strip of light was showing in the east. It spread, glimmering across the mist along the Danube and catching the church spires and steeples – and as the light warmed to a golden glow it sheened the roof tiles and sparkled on windows, and the mist dispelled until it became no more than a soft gossamer veil drawn across the sky.

Paul stooped down and picked a tiny purple flower jewelled by the morning mist. The first of the March violets. 'To match your eyes,' he said.

She took it and cradled it in her hands.

'You know,' he said quietly, 'that Napoleon intends to fight, and that I shall have to go away for a while?'

Lottie's heart turned over. She had known it would have to come. Only not yet.

'But we can go home and be married first?' her voice was unconsciously pleading.

He took the flower and tucked it into her hair.

'The devil himself couldn't keep me from that particular date, lovely Lottie!' he said softly. 'And Napoleon Bonaparte certainly won't!'